JONNY JAKES
Investigates

TH M

Published in the United States in 2016 by Stone Arch Books,
A Capstone Imprint
1710 Roe Crest Drive
North Mankato, Minnesota 56003
www.mycapstone.com

First published in 2015 by Curious Fox,
an imprint of Capstone Global Library Limited
264 Banbury Road, Oxford, OX2 7DY
Registered company number 6695582
www.curious-fox.com

Library of Congress Cataloging-in-Publication Data is available on
the Library of Congress website.

ISBN: 978-1-4965-2678-6 (library binding)
ISBN: 978-1-4965-2680-9 (paperback)
ISBN: 978-1-4965-2681-6 (eBook PDF)

Illustrated by Alan Brown - Advocate Art

Printed and bound in the USA.
009746R

THE HAMBURGERS OF DOOM

Malcolm Judge

capstone

To Kate, Mum, Gregory,
Elliot, and Ollie

I'm Jonny Jakes.

But that's not my real name.

When you're an undercover journalist, you don't use your own name. If you're deep undercover, you don't even use your own hair.

I have three spy cameras, fifteen disguises, and more wigs than is usually considered healthy for a twelve-year-old boy.

I'm the reporter for
The Woodford Word.
Some people call it
the unofficial school
newspaper.

I call it ten pages of
truth and justice.

Mr. Hardy, our principal, thinks *The Woodford Word* is "scurrilous, misleading, and unsuitable for young minds."

That's the thanks you get for telling it like it is.

He's promised pizza parties, ice cream socials, and other tempting rewards to kids that can dig up any information that might lead to the unmasking of Jonny Jakes or the mysterious editor of *The Woodford Word*, Fiona Friend.

My other name is Fiona Friend.

If you want to read about how the school "allows students' creativity to flourish in a supportive environment," then pick up one of the school's glossy brochures. It has a picture on the front of our student senate president pretending to laugh at one of Mr. Hardy's jokes.

If you want to know how the school really works, then pick up a paper.

Mr. Hardy would prefer you'd pick up a brochure.

He doesn't like me.

I think some of my headlines might have offended him:

THE WOODFORD WORD

LARDY HARDY CALLS FOR CARROT CAKE CRACKDOWN

In another act of complete hypocrisy, Lardy Hardy, who only the other day was seen wolfing down a huge

THE WOODFORD WORD

HARDY HARDLY IN CONTROL

Under-fire Hardy has another fight on his hands as what

THE WOODFORD WORD

MOODY HARDY MAD AT MUDDY FEET

Another week, another whine from bumbling principal, Mr. Hardy, as kids are stopped in their muddy tracks. Hardy is

To be honest, I can see why.

Not all of my headlines are about Mr. Hardy. After all, *The Woodford Word*'s mission is to provide students with balanced reporting on every aspect of school life.

It's just that Mr. Hardy asks for it.

Take today. Up until last week, Mr. Hardy's bald spot was big enough to blind low-flying aircraft. This morning he walked in with shiny black hair.

So I'm going with:

THE WOODFORD WORD

HOW COME HARDY'S HAIRY?

In a bald move, hairless principal, Mr. Hardy, has suddenly become Hairy Hardy

I mean, what am I supposed to do? Pretend it didn't happen? My readers demand integrity. I'm a defender of truth and justice.

And I have a paper to sell.

Dictionary Day

Or to give it a proper description:

DIK-shuh-ner-ee DAY (noun) — the day upon
which a dictionary is celebrated

Hardy went ballistic.

He ordered bag searches across the whole school.
Usually I'm pretty careful, but today I had some new
material for the paper badly hidden in my geography
textbook.

I was in English when it happened, Mrs. McKeane's
class. I'm good at English. I just try to make sure
Mrs. McKeane never finds out.

I was sitting next to Norris. Norris Morris. He's only
eleven and he's already the biggest kid in school.
Which is a good thing with a name like that.

Mrs. McKeane announced that she would be inspecting
our backpacks, row by row, and anyone found with
anything they shouldn't have would be sent straight

to the principal's. She was very thorough. Books were shaken, bags were turned upside down, and every copy of *The Woodford Word* was removed and thrown into a black trash bag.

I was trapped.

I quickly looked beneath the table. My bag was open, and there, sticking out of *The Planet We Live On*, was the picture I'd taken of Ms. Frustup's bumper. Her car had mysteriously gotten a dent in it at exactly the same time the NO ENTRY sign at the front of school had gotten knocked over.

All the teachers were blaming it on "local youths," but I knew differently:

THE WOODFORD WORD

FRUSTUP'S BUST-UP

Felicity Frustup, Woodford's pickiest math teacher, seems to have gotten her own angles wrong this time

It was investigative journalism at its finest, and it was about to get me chucked out of school.

Next to my bag, by a pair of huge feet, was Norris's bag. It was also open. I looked up. Mrs. McKeane was getting closer. Trying not to think about the surgery I would need if Norris's boots ever connected with my backside, I reached beneath the desk and slid my textbook and its deadly contents into Norris's bag.

Mrs. McKeane reached our row. She raked her bitter and twisted eyes over us. I tried to act normal, but she was staring so hard that everyone was starting to look like they'd done something wrong.

Everyone, that is, except Norris.

Norris smiled.

Norris always smiles. That's why everyone thinks he's slow.

Mrs. McKeane thought Norris was slow — that's why he was in the back row with me. I could see what she was thinking. Why waste time searching the bags of intellectual pond life when none of us would be able to read *The Woodford Word*, let alone write it?

With a cluck of her tongue, she made up her mind. She spun on her heel and headed back to her favorites at the front of the class and back to Act 3, Scene 5 of *Romeo and Juliet*.

I was free to write another day.

I'd completely forgotten about Norris until a large hand tapped me on the shoulder during lunch.

I turned around slowly. My eyes drew level with a large, white-shirted stomach. I looked up to see a bristly chin and the twin black holes of two giant nostrils. Although it was hard to tell from the angle I was looking from, I was pretty sure Norris was smiling.

I had no idea if that was a good sign or a bad sign.

Norris reached into his pocket and began to pull out some rolled-up paper. It looked very familiar. I said goodbye to the world and shut my eyes.

When nothing happened, I opened my eyes again. Norris's smile had grown even bigger than normal.

"'Frustup's Bust-up.' Nice one," the giant boy said. Then he winked a huge eye and strode off across the playground.

It's amazing I got through the day without needing a change of underwear.

Wednesday, October 17th
Wear Something Gaudy Day
So, no action needed from the Art Department.

Hardy's on his way out! He's had enough.

I haven't even been here a whole semester.

I found out while waiting for the school nurse. I'm a pro at waiting for the nurse. No one bothers me. I put my head in my hands and make a sort of moaning sound. It's like you're invisible.

The great thing about waiting for the nurse is that you get to overhear everything Mrs. Singh says. She's Mr. Hardy's secretary in the next office over. She's so loud you could probably overhear her in the neighboring town.

I get most of my stories while waiting for the nurse and "accidentally" overhearing Mrs. Singh.

As I held my stomach and made the occasional groan, I could hear Mrs. Singh on the phone. (I'm still not convinced she actually needs one.) Her door was closed and I could tell she was trying to keep her voice down, but I still heard more than enough:

> . . . place an ad . . . needs to include an interview date . . . application forms available from . . .

And the clincher:

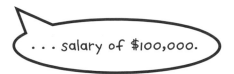

... salary of $100,000.

Only one job at Woodford School earns that kind of
money.

It's time for a special issue.

I can't decide on a headline — there are so many to
choose from:

> ## HARDY HITS THE HIGHWAY

or

> ## HAPPY END TO HARDY HORROR

or

> ## NO MORE HARDY, LET'S PARTY!

I could use the picture I took of kids from the back of a
bus at the start of fall break. It's perfect. They have their

faces all smashed up against the windows and they're waving with their thumbs in their ears.

I could have a "Classic Quotes" section from Mr. Hardy's assemblies, including my all-time favorite:

"This school is a happy school, a caring school, and if I ever find out who stole our framed Positive Learning Environment Gold Star certificate from outside the cafeteria, I'll make them wish they'd never been born."

But that's only two pages.

I need someone to help me find some more material. Someone who won't arouse suspicion. Someone who won't give me away. Someone who won't mind using a silly name.

One particular someone comes to mind.

Thursday, October 18th

The good news is that the special edition broke all the paper's sales records.

The bad news is if I wasn't Public Enemy Number One before, I sure am now.

The teachers are mad that I found out about Hardy leaving before them. Mr. Hardy's mad because the teachers are mad. And now the parents have *gone* mad.

They think *The Woodford Word* has become a menace. They think the school is out of control. They're demanding that Jonny Jakes and Fiona Friend be silenced immediately.

I don't want to be silenced.

Everyone's trying to catch me. Teachers are patrolling up and down the halls, there are random bag checks all the time, and the photocopier rooms are locked after every use.

I need to be careful.

Mrs. McKeane keeps looking at me funny. Maybe I got a little carried away with my essay on *Romeo and Juliet* and forgot to put in enough mistakes. Maybe she's wondering how *The Woodford Word* found out about her forgetting the silent "t" in Mr. De Toillet's name last week.

Or maybe I have GUILTY written all over my face.

Luckily, no one suspects Norris. No one ever suspects Norris. He just keeps smiling at everyone.

He must be the only kid who hasn't had his bag checked, so he's keeping a bunch of photos safe for me. I might not be getting a paper out anytime soon, but when I do, I'm going to have plenty to say about this brutal suppression of free speech.

I'm thinking:

TEACHERS CAN'T TAKE THE TRUTH

Or maybe even:

TRUTH TRAMPLED IN TERRIFYING REIGN OF TEACHER TERROR

Although that's probably overdoing the Ts.

And then there's the damage to the business. The loyalty of my customers. Too many bag searches and they'll turn on me.

Or they would if they knew who I was.

No paper means no profit. No profit means no more disguises. No more disguises means no more wigs.

I must be strong.

Friday, October 19th
Evaluate Your Life Day
Really?

Someone wants to join *The Woodford Word*.

Norris found the sticky note stuck under a teacher's desk in French. The undersides of the French teachers' desks are the communication network of the entire student population. I mean, when was the last time you saw a French teacher look closely at the bottom of their desk?

Exactly.

Dear Fiona Friend,

Would like to help.
Please leave instructions
here tomorrow a.m.

Justin Case

It could be a trap. Mr. Hardy's always trying to trip me up and catch me red-handed. So I'll give Justin Case a challenge. I'll ask him to wait for the nurse and see if he can find out the names of people applying for Hardy's job.

It's about time someone else was sick.

Just to be safe, I'll get Norris to put a reply under a

different desk. If Justin Case is serious, he'll find it. If he doesn't, he doesn't belong on *The Woodford Word*.

Turns out Justin Case *is* serious.

Norris left our note during first period and by lunch he picked up a reply.

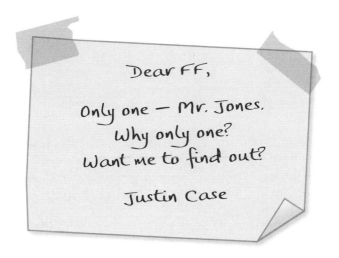

Dear FF,

Only one — Mr. Jones.
Why only one?
Want me to find out?

Justin Case

Only one candidate for a job worth $100,000?

And *Mr. Jones*? What kind of a name is that? That's the kind of name you use when you have to make up a fake name.

I should know.

There's a story here, a big one. Too big to give to some idiot who calls themselves Justin Case.

Saturday, October 20th

Falcon FX 3 released on PlayStation.

Why am I so poor?

I'm hiding in the bathroom.

The relatives are visiting.

I want to keep running with the story, but my Uncle Jack is determined to teach me how to golf. He keeps making me swing an imaginary golf club around my head while he shouts at me to concentrate and keep my eye on the imaginary ball. It's not going very well because all I can think about is wrapping a non-imaginary golf club around his non-imaginary stupid neck.

When I'm not being forced to play imaginary golf, I'm supposed to be playing with my two-year-old cousin.

He doesn't want to play with me.

He just wants to gnaw on my ankles.

Sunday, October 21st

See yesterday.

Monday, October 22nd

As soon as I finished breakfast, I went straight over to Norris's house. We made up three people to apply for Mr. Hardy's job. I only have three accents.

There was Mr. Jackson from Texas, Mr. Rossini from New York, and Mr. O'Malley from Ireland.

Norris made me practice. Mr. Jackson sounded okay, Mr. Rossini was kind of sketchy, and Mr. O'Malley kept sounding like a hyper leprechaun.

It's a good thing I didn't get to say much. All three conversations with Mrs. Singh went exactly like this:

> Good morning, I'm Mr. Jackson/Rossini/ O'Malley. I'd like an application for the position of Principal at Woodford School, please.

> I'm sorry, sir, but the position has already been filled. *Click.*

It was really weird for two reasons:

1. The ad only just appeared in the paper and the final date for applications was two weeks away. Since when do you give someone the job and *then* advertise it?

2. (And this was the really weird one) Mrs. Singh didn't want to chat.

Mrs. Singh always wants to chat. She once told me the entire life story of her cat.

I'd only asked her for a new planner.

So, not only did just one person apply for the job, it seems like the school only wants one person for the job.

Who is this Mr. Jones and what makes him so special?

Tuesday, October 23rd
Mole Day
Celebrate only if you *really* want everyone to
know how much of science nerd you are.

Mr. Jones is a hard man to track down.

I spent forty minutes at the nurse's office with a funny pain in my elbow and didn't once hear his name mentioned. Norris had a sprained nose for an hour and a half. Nothing.

More advanced research methods were required.

Previous undercover investigations have revealed that every day, at 2 p.m. precisely, Mrs. Singh takes a big red bag full of mail across the playground to the post office across from the school.

So, today at 1:59 and 55 seconds, a guy who looked a little like me, only with curly hair, three large moles,  and gigantic ears, threw a ball high into the air. As luck would have it, the ball happened to travel in the direction of the large double doors leading out from the school's front office to the playground.

Norris, being an enthusiastic athlete, was determined to make the catch and backpedaled quickly after the ball.

At 1:59 and 59 seconds, Norris made a great catch.

At 2 p.m. precisely, his backward momentum propelled him into a lady with a big red bag.

At 2 p.m. and 3 seconds, I arrived on the scene to help.

I helped pick up letters to parents, payments for bills, and order forms for stationery. I also picked up a small white envelope addressed to a Mr. Jones, which I completely forgot to put back in the big red bag.

At the end of our afternoon break, as everyone drifted back to class, Norris and I drifted to the tin-roofed shed that stored all the sports equipment. Once we were safely out of sight, I took off my disguise and got the white envelope out of my pocket.

I knew that you could use steam from a kettle to open sealed envelopes without it looking too sketchy, but I didn't have a kettle, so I tried breathing on it instead.

I hadn't gotten very far when Norris snatched the envelope out of my hands and ripped it in half.

"Norris, w-what the . . ." I stammered, flabbergasted.

Then Norris stamped on the torn up envelope and smiled.

"What are you smiling at, you moron?" I shouted at him. In my panic, I'd forgotten I was yelling at the biggest kid in school.

Norris's smile widened and then he pretended to look innocent.

"Sorry, ma'am," he said, putting on a goody-goody voice and perfect puppy-dog eyes. "This must have fallen out of your bag. I think it must have gotten stuck on my boot."

It took a moment or so to register, but that's when I realized that Norris Morris — the stupid, smiling giant of Woodford School — was in fact a genius.

I joined the two halves of the letter together, took a picture, and then started to read.

Woodford School
West Woodford, MA

Mr. Jones
PO Box 4571
Boston, MA 02114

Dear Mr Jones,

Thank you for your gracious acceptance of the position of Principal at Woodford School. I can't tell you how excited we all are. Everything is going smoothly. I look forward to meeting you in my office at 7:30 Thursday morning, as arranged, so we can make our final plans and I can answer any further questions you might have.

Yours sincerely,

Geoffrey Hardy

I was about to say something when a high-pitched voice behind me beat me to it.

"Give it!"

We turned around. Michelle Bell, the toughest girl in school, held out her hand. There was a big gold ring on every finger. They weren't for decoration.

In our rush, we hadn't checked to make sure that we were alone. Rookie mistake. A pro like me should've known better.

Michelle Bell wasn't alone. She never was. She and Trevor Neave were going steady — he was sharing his bag of Doritos with her.

"Hey! Hand it over. Or . . ." Trevor Neave paused. He could barely speak in sentences, let alone write them. "Else!" he finally managed.

I had no problem handing over the letter. There wasn't exactly a whole lot to remember, so why not let someone else run the risk of getting caught with it?

Norris, however, had other ideas. I'd never seen him without a smile before now.

"Or else what?" he said in a steely voice.

Trevor Neave unwrapped his hairy arms from the tiny waist of Michelle Bell and squared up to Norris. He may have been stupid, but he recognized a challenge to his position as the school tough guy when he saw it.

At any other time, I would have happily stepped back and watched Norris pound Trevor Neave into a pulp, but we had bigger fish to fry. Besides, Jonny Jakes works better in the shadows and he was in serious danger of stepping into the limelight.

Trevor Neave was gearing up for another attempt at intelligent speech, but I saved him the effort.

"Take it," I said, holding the letter toward him. "Be my guest. We'll leave you to it."

I pulled at Norris's sleeve, but he was failing to grasp the idea of not drawing attention to ourselves. He was failing to grasp it in a spectacular way.

"No!" Norris said, snatching the letter out of my hand again. He was red in the face. "We need this. It's too important. We need it for the paper . . ."

To be fair, as soon as he'd said it, he realized what he'd done. Unfortunately, he was one word too late.

Michelle Bell placed her bright-red fingernails on Trevor Neave's shoulder and gently pulled him out of the way. She had a vicious smile on her face.

"The paper?" she trilled annoyingly. "So, you losers work for *The Woodford Word*? How interesting."

I thought about trying to deny it, but Norris's face was a complete giveaway. So I did the next best thing. I kept quiet. Better her thinking we were a tiny cog in the machine rather than her knowing that we *were The Woodford Word*.

"Cat got your tongue?" she continued, spinning a blob of bubble gum around her mouth. "Well, that's okay, losers. I'll do the talking for you. You tell Fiona Friend that I want my own fashion feature. It's about time that paper had something good in it. Tell her I want a full spread with glossy pictures and fashion advice. And tell her I want to be called . . . Chella. Do you think you can remember all that, losers?"

I nodded. I tried to bite my tongue.

It didn't work.

"And what if Fiona Friend tells you to go stick your head down a toilet?"

Michelle Bell leaned in close. I could barely breathe because of all her nasty perfume.

"Then tell her," she whispered, "that if I don't see myself in print by the end of this week, two of her reporters will be expelled."

And with those kind words, she left, pulling her boyfriend along by his tie.

Norris stared at the muddy paper in his hands. He looked like he'd never smile again.

Wednesday, October 24th
Switzerland becomes independent, 1648
I still have to wait another seven years.

I need to get *The Woodford Word* out by Friday or I'm done for.

The problem is the teachers are everywhere, marching up and down the halls, invading the playground, and generally lurking around every corner. My bag gets searched about five times a day, and if Mrs. McKeane stares at me any harder, she's going to go cross-eyed.

Norris hasn't been much help. I can't get a word out of him. I tried complimenting him and I tried shouting at him. As a last resort, I tried hitting him, but I don't think he even noticed that. He's like a zombie. If he doesn't start smiling soon, he's going to get his bag inspected like the rest of us.

Then, even if I do get the paper out, it has to have a full-spread fashion feature put together by someone who wouldn't know fashion if it jumped out and catwalked across her face.

The one consolation is the Mr. Jones letter.

It's a pretty big consolation. Intrigue, conspiracy, and double-dealing — it doesn't get much better than that. And guess where I'm going to be at 7:30 tomorrow morning?

Thursday, October 25th

At last. The story that will make me a legend.

This time I'm not just going to make the headlines. I'm going to *be* the headlines.

World domination of the media ☑

I left home early. Mom wasn't even awake yet. I put a note under her door telling her I'd probably be back late because I had a ton of homework I needed to finish at school. She falls for it every time.

Me and Norris had to find a good hiding place before the meeting. For the first half of the semester, I'd been skulking around the hall outside of Hardy's office. Today I was going in.

Our disguises were simple but effective: coveralls and baseball hats. We could have been stocking up the vending machine, moving some furniture, or cleaning the drains. No one would give us a second thought, and the bills on our hats meant our faces wouldn't be seen by the security cameras trained on the school entrance.

Lucky for us, Hardy's door was unlocked. It was a big, towering wooden door and it creaked dramatically as we pushed it open. I bet he deliberately doesn't oil the hinges.

I put my finger on my lips and we went in.

Our luck stopped as soon as it started. Mr. Hardy's office is probably the most boring office in the whole wide world. Apart from the hideous wallpaper, there was just a big desk, three chairs, and a steel storage cabinet.

The storage cabinet might have worked as a hiding place, but it was locked and we couldn't find the key. We tried under the desk, but Norris kept lifting it up with his massive butt.

As Norris crawled back out from under the desk, he pointed to his watch to show me that we were running out of time.

I pointed to his huge backside to explain why our plan was experiencing a little difficulty.

He did a little mime to suggest that we go up on the roof so that he could lower me down to watch through the top of Mr. Hardy's window.

I did a little mime to show him that, actually, I had completely forgotten to bring my climbing rope with me.

Norris did a mime back that suggested I was just a big chicken and that if I didn't get up the drainpipe right now, he was going to tell everyone.

I started to do a mime back, but Norris didn't like it and made me stop.

We booked it back outside, around to the side of the school, and scrambled up the drainpipe that Matthew Robinson uses when the jocks make him get their footballs off the roof. No sooner were we up on the roof tiles when we heard a car rumbling into the parking lot.

It was Hardy. He got out directly below us. He must've really been trying to impress his mysterious visitor.

His wig was freshly washed, and as we peeked a little farther over the edge of the roof, we could almost see our reflection in his perfectly polished shoes.

Minutes later another car arrived. Something was off about it.

I tried to figure out what was so weird. Was it too black? Was it too quiet? Or was it because it didn't seem to completely make contact with the ground?

I looked at Norris. He was as puzzled as me.

The car silently pulled to a halt next to Hardy's. I still didn't recognize the make or model. There was no hood ornament or name on it. And there were no lines on it either, absolutely nothing to help you tell the difference between the doors or the hood or the windshield. It looked like it was made from a solid piece of pure black.

A door opened. Norris and I held our breath. At last we were going to see our mysterious new principal. A brown shoe stepped out onto the pavement, then another.

Then another.

But before we could
see any more,
Mr. Hardy blocked
our view by opening
up an umbrella
over his guest and
whisking him inside.
I'd been too stunned
to even think about
taking a photograph
until it was too late.

All I got was the top of the umbrella.

My heart was racing. I held up three fingers to Norris,
just to make sure my brain hadn't made it up. He held
up three fingers back and nodded.

Once we'd given them a little time to get settled,
Norris grabbed my ankles and carefully lowered me
headfirst over the edge of the roof. The blood rushed
to my head and I could feel Norris trembling with
the effort of holding me. I should have been scared,

but the smell of a big story has a way of keeping me focused.

Inch by inch, my eyes drew level with the top edge of Mr. Hardy's window. My eyes widened. If I hadn't been held upside down by the biggest kid in school, I'd have fainted with the shock.

I'm not quite sure how to say this, so I'm just going to say it.

. . . It's probably best to sit down.

Mr. Jones is an alien.

I know. It still sounds weird to me and I *saw* it. I've been practicing saying it in my head all day.

Mr. Jones is an alien.

Still weird.

But he is. Either that or the human race has just evolved into three-legged, purple-headed, five-eyed beings and I just didn't notice.

And this time I did get a picture.

I think it's safe to say we've got a front page.

I made sure Norris put me down safely before I told him what I'd seen. I had to tell him a few times.

He wanted to have a look for himself, but I wasn't about to try and dangle him off the edge of a building, so he had to make do with the photograph I'd taken. Eventually it seemed to sink in.

Mr. Jones's exit was as quick as his arrival. Mr. Hardy held the umbrella over his head again, despite the bright sunshine. As far as the two of them were concerned, they'd just had a secret meeting.

They'll soon find out they didn't.

We spent the rest of the morning in a daze. I think I might have even smiled at Michelle Bell as she handed over *The Woodford Word*'s new fashion feature. It had lots of pictures of her friends trying on dresses with too many straps.

By lunch I'd managed to clear my head a little, so I started thinking about how we were actually going to get the paper out. Online has never been an option. I never know when I'm going to get banned. Besides, the internet speed at school makes the average snail look like a Formula One race car.

Trying to get access to a photocopier would be impossible — they were too heavily guarded. We needed to get a hold of a whole bunch of printer ink and paper and then find a nice, quiet room with a computer, a scanner, and a printer. It had to be somewhere nobody ever goes, where we could work without interruption. We'd also have to stay in the room for a very long time.

Which is why we're still in the PE study room.

Friday, October 26th
National Pumpkin Day
Soon to be followed by Massacre a Pumpkin Day, AKA Halloween.

By the end of today, I should have been rich and famous beyond my wildest dreams — and I have some pretty wild dreams.

Norris and I had everything ready to go. We had worked through the night, chugging down cups of coffee and cans of Mountain Dew. By the time we heard the janitor doing his early morning rounds, there were five hundred copies of *The Woodford Word* ready to shock the world.

We kept the headline simple, but we put it twice:

THE WOODFORD WORD

NEW PRINCIPAL OF WOODFORD SCHOOL IS AN ALIEN
NEW PRINCIPAL OF WOODFORD SCHOOL IS AN ALIEN

After all, with a story like that and a picture to back it up, what else did we need?

We sneaked out of the PE study room with our bundles of papers. Yesterday Norris had put a note under Madame Angerie's desk to let everyone know that, despite the ongoing danger of our secret identities being revealed, we had a story that just had to be told. It informed kids that copies of *The Woodford Word* would be available first thing Friday morning in lockers 501 and 502, and they didn't even have to pay for it.

We didn't notice anything at first. But when we saw a clock, I realized something was up. It was 8:35 and it was quiet.

Too quiet.

We listened carefully for signs of life. There was a faint hum coming from the direction of the auditorium. Every now and then it would rise up before bubbling down again.

Norris and I started to walk toward it.

As we got closer, the sound changed. It was more broken up and getting louder. It was the sound of voices, hundreds of voices, all chattering at the same time. Sometimes the voices would gather into a wave of noise, and when it did, we could make out cheers and clapping.

Something big was going on. I got a funny feeling in the pit of my stomach and it had nothing to do with me missing breakfast.

I happened to look out of one of the hall windows and

saw a row of white vans parked along the road leading up to the school. They had antennae and satellite dishes sticking out the top of them.

That wasn't normal.

I looked closer and saw cameras and lots of people with headphones talking to lots of other people with headphones. There were even a couple of helicopters circling above.

By the time we got to the auditorium, the sound had reached a fever pitch. Norris managed to push open the double doors just wide enough for us to slip into the excited crowd.

Everyone was trying to get a view of the stage. I could see some of the kids in my grade sitting on top of their dads' shoulders and every window ledge and every chair was being stood on. I could hardly see a thing. One of Norris's more useful skills as an undercover reporter is that he's strong enough to let you stand on his shoulders while he grabs your legs.

On the stage was a single microphone lit by a single spotlight. Just when it seemed like the noise couldn't get any louder, there was a violent shushing sound as everyone put their fingers to their lips. Mr. Hardy came on the stage. He tried his best to look serious, but you could tell he was loving all the attention.

He waited until every last whisper had died before he started to speak.

"Ladies and gentlemen, welcome to Woodford School. As you know, the school has always been at the cutting edge of education, and today is no different.

"Today, we break more boundaries and tread new ground. Children, parents, ladies and gentlemen of the press, I'm afraid we have been keeping a little secret from you. Indeed, we've been keeping it from the rest of the world. A secret that even *The Woodford Word* hasn't managed to uncover."

He paused for dramatic effect. I wanted to yell something, anything, but my throat was completely dry. This wasn't supposed to happen.

"Today, Woodford School begins a project that will pave the way for the teaching of tomorrow."

Mr. Hardy paused again. He'd spent a lot of time coming up with that.

"We've been doing our own homework, and through our extensive search for a new principal, we've discovered that, in order to provide our children with a world-class education, we needed something that's, well, a little out of this world."

The funny feeling in the pit of my stomach was feeling less funny all the time, and my brain had turned to mush. My world exclusive was about to slip through my fingers, and all I could do was stand there and watch.

Mr. Hardy was working up to his finale.

"Ladies and gentlemen, I
never thought I'd be the
one to tell you, indeed
to tell the world, that
we are not alone in the
universe. But it is my
great honor to introduce
you to a teacher who has come a very long way to be
with us today. A teacher whose skills have been honed
in classrooms not just across the country, but across
the cosmos. A teacher who not only knows the square
root of pi, but uses it to steer his spacecraft. Ladies and
gentlemen, from the planet Huurl, please welcome . . .
Mr. Jones."

And there he was.

All three legs, five eyes, and purple head of him.

And in lockers 501 and 502, five hundred newspapers
just became yesterday's news.

Saturday, October 26th

Where's the end of
the world when you need it?

Yesterday I had the chance to break the biggest
news story since dinosaurs were wiped off the face of
the earth.

And I blew it.

Mr. Jones's face is everywhere. You can't move an inch
without hearing his name. You know when something
really important has happened when everyone forgets
to talk about the weather.

He's all over the TV, all over the radio, and the
internet is in serious risk of a meltdown. What makes
it worse is that most of the time Hardy's there too.
Last week he was on the front of *The Woodford Word*
stuffing his face with a bunch of cake, now he's on the
cover of the *New York Times* with his arm around Mr.
Jones, smiling like he just won a lifetime supply of
Twinkies.

I think I'm going to have to spend the rest of my life under a rock.

 Sunday, October 27th

I haven't left my bedroom all weekend.

Mom's been trying to lure me out with cake. She says I'll feel better after some fresh air and a good talk.

Dad keeps knocking on my door and asking me to turn the awful music down. I can't believe I'm related to someone who doesn't appreciate the musical genius of The Pain Cradle.

Norris stopped by to say I should be happy with how close we got to the story of a lifetime. He said I have a great future ahead of me and I should stop sulking and pull myself together.

I told him to go away and stop talking like my parents.

First, you find out your new principal is an alien.

Then, your old principal tells the world about it just before you do and ruins the rest of your life. Then, as if things weren't bad enough already, the new principal calls a special assembly in the gym, which means you have to sit on a cold wooden floor and get talked at. For an hour.

Mr. Jones came into the gym accompanied by a barrage of flash photography from the world's press who haven't found anything better to do with themselves yet. He was wearing the same stuff as before: brown suit, brown and white striped tie, white shirt, brown pants, and brown shoes. I don't know if he thinks that's what an Earth teacher should wear, or whether the rest of the universe just has no style.

Up close, you could see that his five eyes were able to look in five different directions at once and that he smelled a little like dishwater. He fit right in with the Chemistry Department.

But the worst thing about it all wasn't the press, or his smell, or my numb butt on the cold floor. It wasn't even his appalling fashion sense.

The worse thing about it was that he was so nice.

He started with a little talk of "firm but fair" and "running a tight ship," but then he started apologizing that we hadn't been told about him before. He said that he'd asked Mr. Hardy if he could let the students know as soon as the school had first contacted him, but he'd been persuaded not to. He hoped he could "earn our trust" in the weeks to follow. He showed us where his home planet was and some pictures of schools in other galaxies that he'd worked in. He showed us a picture of his personal spaceship and some pictures of his children.

He has seventy-three.

He kept saying "what a privilege" it was to be here and how much he was looking forward to "learning together." At the end, he even offered everyone some candy.

It was so bad, I almost wished Mr. Hardy was back.

When it was all over, I tried standing up, but my brain had forgotten what my legs did, so I just stayed where I was. Everyone else looked pretty dazed, too, as they wandered to their classes. Some kids even waited around to ask him questions.

Mr. Jones smiled patiently and answered them all, one by one.

I hate him.

I don't know how long I was like that, just sitting and staring and wishing I could wipe the stupid triangular smile off his stupid purple face. If Norris hadn't poked me in the ribs, I'd probably still be there now.

I'm depressed.

I'm spending so much time in my bedroom that I've started naming the furniture.

Tuesday, October 29th
The anniversary of the start of
the Great Depression
I know how they felt.

Justin Case is at it again.

Norris brought me a note at lunch.

Dear FF,

Why didn't you get back to me?
I found his name out, didn't I? We
could have gotten to this story first.
We could have been famous!
Thanks for nothing!

JC

It was nice to know someone else was in a bad mood,
but it didn't help cheer me up.

Wednesday, October 30th

I must be pretty bad. I heard Mom ask Dad if he could have a father-and-son talk with me about how my body was changing and how to control my emotions.

I hope he keeps it short.

Norris brought me three more notes from Justin Case today; they kind of have a theme.

Dear FF,

I didn't mean to get angry, it's just I'm sure we could make a good team, that's all. Look, I've found out something else that you'll find interesting. Get back to me by lunch and I might just let you in on a little secret!

JC

FF,

So you're just going to ignore me now? Well, don't think I'm going anywhere. If you won't keep up with the news, then I will. If I don't get a note by the end of the day, then *The Woodford Word* is history — I'll start my own paper.

JC

Hey, FF!
Or whatever your stupid name is.

I mean it! You're either with me or against me!! I'm not bluffing!!!

JC

He's bluffing.

If you're serious, you don't need to use three exclamation marks.

Thursday, October 31st

Halloween
Definitely the last year my Dracula
costume's going to fit me.

The reporters are starting to drift off. It's easy reporting on the arrival of the first extra-terrestrial life form, but it's difficult to keep writing articles about how nice he is. Mr. Jones has been giving them regular briefings. I've been to a few in disguise.

Someone made the mistake of asking him what it was like to teach human students. He went on and on about the joys of teaching ultra-long division to the sixth graders, how ninth graders were fascinated by the fundamentals of Huurlian grammar, and what an incredibly interesting game baseball is.

It's gotten to the point where all they ask him now is whether they can have some more of his candy.

Friday, November 1st

Everyone still loves Mr. Jones. It's making me crazy. Okay, so he's got a brain the size of a planet and he's taught us more in one week than we've learned in the whole rest of our education.

But that's not the point.

He's everywhere. You can't get away from him. He glides through the halls, and he's so quick and quiet. It's unnerving.

I had my head in my locker today, getting my books out, and when I turned around — *boom*! There he was, right in front of me. Smiling.

He's even worse than Norris with his smiling.

He offered me one of his candies and asked me if I was okay. I said I was fine, but my stomach just felt a little funny. His eyes were all full of understanding, or at least the three that I could see were. I thought for a second that he might have figured out who I was, but he seemed genuinely upset that I didn't seem happy. I couldn't tell him my problem was staring me in the face.

I can't have teachers feeling sorry for me.

The Woodford Word must rise again.

Saturday, November 2nd

I'm trying to work on the paper. There's just one problem.

No news.

Everything's been perfect this week. No one's missing class or coming in late. The school looks cleaner than ever. All the teachers are being nice and all the kids are really happy.

Well, nearly all.

Why is everyone being so nice? Even Trevor Neave's managed to stop hitting people.

Other than having an alien for a principal, the only story is there is no story.

 Sunday, November 3rd

Mr. Jones did one of those interviews-on-a-couch type talk shows on TV this morning. He was asked what he was enjoying most about life on Earth. He said he didn't think much of the weather, but he couldn't believe how he'd managed to survive so long without a decent cup of coffee. The interviewer laughed his head off.

I almost cried.

I'm starting a report on Mr. Jones. I might have to publish it if I can't find anything to put in the paper.

I'm brainstorming titles. The two I like right now are:

MR. JONES
The Truth About The Thing
That Ruined My Life

or

EXTRA-TERRESTRIAL LIFE
More Boring Than You
Would Have Ever Thought Possible

Monday, November 4th

I knew Justin Case was bluffing.

Dear FF,

All right, so I was bluffing. I just want to help. Something's wrong. I did some investigating. Mr. Jones doesn't get paid, not even in alien money. I don't get it — what's in it for him??? Give me a chance.

JC

I don't like his name and I definitely don't like his excessive use of punctuation, but Justin Case is digging up some pretty good stuff.

I don't get it either. Who travels halfway across the universe just out of the goodness of his heart, especially when he has seventy-three mouths to feed?

Maybe I should give Justin Case a chance. I can't afford not to have the kind of information he keeps coming up with.

It's a good thing I finally have some sort of story. Michelle Bell cornered me at my locker between classes.

She was a little calmer than usual but still wanted to know what had happened to her fashion feature.

I tried to explain that Fiona Friend had put her fashion feature in the last edition of *The Woodford Word*, but after Mr. Jones showed up, no one had wanted to buy it. That only started to wind her up again. So then I tried to point out that it was really hard to get a paper out right now because everyone was being so nice to each other.

I have three days to work it out or something horrible is going to happen to my leg.

Tuesday, November 5th
Election Day
If only kids got to vote for their principals.

I left a note for Justin Case explaining how our business relationship would work.

JC,

If you want to help *The Woodford Word,* stop using so much punctuation, or I will make it my mission in life to reveal your true identity and take you down.

FF
P.S. Dig deeper

Then Norris and I went alien-tracking.

We watched Mr. Jones's every move.

We stalked him down the halls and saw him ask some ninth graders to tuck in their shirts. We spied on him in the faculty lounge with a camera we'd hidden behind the teachers' mailboxes and heard him ask Mrs. Flynn how her mother was. We watched through the window near the Music Department as he patrolled the playground and kicked a soccer ball back to Simon Huck after he'd missed a penalty kick.

We saw him do nothing suspicious whatsoever.

By the end of the day, I was exhausted and beginning to think I should forget the whole thing. Maybe I'd gotten it all wrong. Maybe it's just humans who want to get paid for working.

I was following Mr. Jones down the millionth hall of the day and wasn't paying attention. I'd gotten way too close. Suddenly he turned around unexpectedly and I nearly walked right into him.

"Sorry, sir, I wasn't watching where I was going," I spluttered. My heart was pounding. I was sure he must have figured out he was being followed. He had enough eyes. But Mr. Jones hardly seemed to notice I was there. He was sucking hard on something in his mouth.

"Don't worry, dear boy, don't worry," he murmured in a distracted sort of way. "Here, have a piece of candy," he said cheerfully and offered me his bag of candy.

That's when it hit me. We'd followed him all day, and he'd given a piece of candy to everyone he met.

Most principals don't do that kind of thing.

Slowly, I put my thoughts together:

1. Mr. Jones has been handing out candy from the second he arrived.

2. Ever since he arrived, everyone's been acting weirdly nice.

3. Something in the candy is making everyone act weirdly nice.

4. Eating Mr. Jones's candy would be a really bad idea for an undercover reporter who needs to stay focused on being a defender of truth and justice.

Luckily, I hadn't had any yet. I don't take candy from strangers, and I certainly don't take it from aliens who've helped destroy my chances of becoming rich and famous beyond my wildest dreams. I had banned Norris from having any, too, on principle. It hadn't gone down well, but he'd thank me now.

The bag of candy came closer. It had a powerful, honey-like smell that made your head spin. I was overcome by the strangest desire to jump inside the bag and swim around in the sugar-coated goodness.

"No, thank you," I said as politely as I could manage.

Mr. Jones was alert in an instant. Most of his eyes stopped whatever it was they were doing and turned to look at me. I felt like an amoeba under a microscope.

"Everyone else likes them," he said, pulling at his lower lip thoughtfully. It wasn't a pretty sight.

I needed an excuse. I'm good at excuses. Normally
I have hundreds of them. But at that moment they
all vanished from my mind. Mr. Jones continued to
examine me.

Finally an excuse popped in my head. It wasn't good,
but it would have to do. Mr. Jones's stare was about to
crumble me into a pile of dust.

"I have to go, sir, it's . . . uh . . . my cat's birthday."

And with that masterpiece, I turned and forced myself
to walk calmly to the end of the hall. I could feel Mr.
Jones's stare, burning into my back the whole time like
five red-hot pinpricks.

As soon as I rounded the corner and was out of sight, I booked it all the way home.

I told my parents about Mr. Jones and his diabolical candy.

They said I had an overactive imagination. They said I should give him a chance and that I just needed a little time to adjust to his methods.

I said what was the point of telling them about my problems if they wouldn't take me seriously.

They said I was jumping to conclusions.

I said they should go jump in a lake.

That's when they sent me to my room.

They came up later for a "chat." Dad sat on my bed and talked in that stupid way he does when he thinks he's treating me like an adult. Mom sat next to him and nodded, but I know she hates that voice too. I can tell by the way she grinds her teeth.

She took over and said they were glad I'd come to them with my concerns and, if it made me feel better, they would promise not to eat any of Mr. Jones's candy.

I thanked her for her concern, but as she left, I caught her giving Dad one of her winks.

I'd take Dad's annoying voice over that wink any day.

Wednesday, November 6th

We're in big trouble. The candy is making everyone in school go around with big, dopey smiles on their face.

Even the teachers.

It's a really weird smile. It looks like it's been painted on by a four-year-old. Everyone's mouth is full of teeth. Their eyes are shiny but kind of glazed-over at the same time, like they're all trying way too hard to look cheerful in a photograph.

I warned Justin Case about the candy. He said he hasn't had any either since he's a diabetic. He doesn't have anything new on Mr. Jones, but he's as freaked out as I am about how everyone's behaving.

The Woodford Word has to bring the school back to its senses. It's time to fire up the photocopier and go for some shock tactics. The headline's going to be:

WHAT ARE YOU LAUGHING AT?

I'm using an old picture of kids on the playground:

It's good to know art class hasn't been a complete waste of time.

Thursday, November 7th

Yesterday I thought we were in trouble.

Today made yesterday look like a walk in the park.

We didn't sell a single copy of *The Woodford Word*. We didn't even manage to give one away.

In the end, we resorted to slipping copies into peoples' bags when they weren't looking, but when they found them, they just picked them up, stared at them blankly, and threw them in the trash. No one was interested.

Apart from Mr. Jones.

He called an all-school assembly.

"Good morning, children," he began. It didn't sound like he meant it.

"Good morning," the grinning zombies chanted back.

"It has come to my attention that some of us are unhappy," he continued, "and if you're unhappy, it makes me unhappy." Mr. Jones sighed for effect. For some reason everyone else did the same. Mr. Jones held up *The Woodford Word* between what we would have called a thumb and a forefinger but which looked more like a stapler and a butter dish.

"I was told about this paper before I arrived. As I'm sure you are aware, my predecessor, Mr. Hardy, was not a fan of this newspaper and warned me to be on the lookout for the students responsible. Well, children, today I am on the lookout for those responsible. Not because I want to punish them, of course, but because I would like to talk with them, to listen to their concerns, and to put their minds at ease."

Something dark swam across the back of Mr. Jones's eyes. He smiled harder.

"As you know, children, I like to recognize the diverse

achievements of every student. If there are some of us who have a talent for . . ." He paused to make sure he chose the right words, and I could tell he was trying to control his temper. ". . . For creative writing, then I would like to discuss how we can work together to develop that talent further.

"So, if Ms. Friend or Mr. Jakes — or indeed anyone else with a delightfully funny name — would like to come visit me in my office, I'm sure we could work out any problems. In the meantime, I suggest we recycle Ms. Friend's contribution in the paper recycling boxes I have just ordered for each classroom."

All three corners of Mr. Jones's mouth were quivering. He was fighting his temper, but his temper was winning.

He was starting to shout as he paced restlessly up and down the stage.

"Of course, if neither Mr. Jakes or Ms. Friend wants to come forward, then one of their friends might need to persuade them! Perhaps there is someone here now who would like to tell us who they really are! Come now, we don't have all day!"

Mr. Jones's normal, smooth movements had become jerky, and his whole barrel chest began heaving violently up and down. When he spoke again, the words struggled to get out.

"The person who tells me . . . gets . . . a . . . bag . . . of CAAAAANNDY!"

Mr. Jones was now completely out of control. His head was swelling up, and as his pacing got faster and faster, his breathing became louder and louder. It was deep and unpleasant and rattly, like someone brushing gravel down a drain.

Then another noise began to fill the hall — a loud, liquidy, pumping sound. The sound of Mr. Jones's heartbeat.

Well, five heartbeats.

I never want to hear anything like it again.

Finally, just in case things weren't totally freaky enough, Mr. Jones's eyes started to dart about.

Literally.

The smallest one moved first. The skin around it just seemed to swim out of the way as the eye went from his forehead to his chin. In a few moments, all the eyes were whirling wildly, pulsating in time with the heartbeats and changing color as they went.

The whole thing was having an effect on the students.

They started to sway on their feet, and their shoulders whipped back and forth. I was so shocked I almost forgot to copy them.

Mr. Jones stepped down from the stage. He started to inspect the rows of horribly shaking bodies.

When he got to Barry Devine, Mr. Jones stopped. Something about him had caught his attention. He slowly circled around the boy, bent over him, and ran his bulging nose up and down his arm. Barry's eyes stared straight ahead, unaware that he now had alien snot dripping off his sleeve.

I tried really hard not to puke.

Just when I felt like there was no holding it back, the doors at the side of the auditorium clattered open. Ms. Briars, the drama teacher, backed into the hall noisily dragging a large table behind her. Mr. Jones's spell was instantly broken and one thousand two hundred and fifty-four kids came back to their senses.

One of them discovered a disgusting new stain on his shirt.

Ms. Briars was halfway across the auditorium before she realized she wasn't alone. When she did, she fumbled for her glasses, which hung on a long piece of gold cord around her neck.

"Oh, sorry, Mr. Jones. Uh . . . kids! School play auditions!" she said, pointing proudly at the table. Mr. Jones didn't say anything. He was doing his best to start breathing normally again, but his face was like a thunderstorm.

After a long, uncomfortable silence, Ms. Briars eventually got the hint that maybe now was not the time. "Well, I'll go back downstairs, then. Everyone's welcome, of course, to . . . you know . . . try out. Umm . . . uh . . . right. Toodle-oo!"

Everyone turned to watch her go, which she did after colliding with a large trash can.

After she left, the whole school turned back to Mr. Jones. A sea of vacant smiles waited for him to say something. They were disappointed.

I'm scrapping the report on Mr. Jones. We need a survival guide. Something like:

> ## A SURVIVAL GUIDE TO ALIENS AND HOW TO ESCAPE THEIR EVIL FIVE-EYED CLUTCHES

I gave my parents a second chance and told them about the assembly.

It was either that or call the police, and I figured my parents were less likely to put me in a straitjacket and cart me off to a padded room.

This time they actually listened. They took me seriously. They said they'd take it up with the school first thing in the morning. Dad said I did the right thing in coming to them. Mom asked me if I was okay and if there was anything I wanted.

I was just beginning to think that they might actually be of some use for a change when they smiled. A shiver ran down my spine.

It was one of *those* smiles.

I asked them if they'd had any candy. They said they didn't, although Mr. Jones had mentioned the candy in the meeting last night.

I said what meeting.

They said the "Meet the Principal" meeting all the moms and dads went to.

Goose bumps sprang up my arm.

They said it was very interesting. They said several parents had asked about the candy and Mr. Jones had admitted he used it to help achieve a "positive learning environment." He also admitted that the candy had a slightly hypnotic quality.

He showed them pictures of how the candy had helped control students' behavior in other schools he'd taught at. They said he'd even admitted giving a few to the press since he'd been told they might be a nuisance and that it would help keep them in order.

They said that Mr. Jones had made it very clear that the candy would be phased out very soon, once "positive

learning patterns have been thoroughly embedded."
The more they talked about him, the bigger their
smiles got.

I asked them again if they were sure they hadn't had
any candy.

They said no.

But the cookies were delicious.

Friday, November 8th

Norris's parents are the same.

He said that when he'd told them about the assembly
at school, they'd listened carefully, just like mine.
He said they'd had a weird smile on their faces, just
like mine. Then he said they'd given him a nice, long
bear hug.

I'd been lucky.

I told Norris we had to send a note to Justin Case to see if he was still okay. I hadn't noticed anyone else who wasn't in a trance in the assembly. Hopefully that was just because I'd been too busy acting like my brains had been sucked out.

Justin Case sent a note back saying he was okay, but he thought *I'd* been got.

I sent a note telling him we were fine but our parents had been got.

He sent a note back saying his were the same and shouldn't we be contacting the authorities.

I sent a note back asking him if he knew the my-principal-is-a-mind-controlling-alien emergency number to call.

He sent a note back saying there's no need to be sarcastic.

Then Norris said he was sick of passing notes back.

"You need to meet him," he added.

"Why?"

"Well, what do we have to lose?" he asked, gulping down the can of Mountain Dew he'd gotten from the grocery store. "Right now it's three of us against all of them and we're spending our time swapping notes instead of actually doing something."

He had a point. To celebrate, he broke the seal on an extra large jar of crunchy peanut butter and dipped his finger in. We can only eat food we buy ourselves now.

I don't think Norris is going to maintain a balanced diet.

"But you need to hide your identity," he said, spraying me with globs of nutty paste.

"But you just said we needed to meet," I said.

"Yeah, but you don't want to *see* each other."

"What do you mean?"

"You don't want to actually see each other because, if one of you gets caught, you'll be forced to tattle on the other guy. If you don't know who the other person is, you can't tattle."

Norris had a point. That made for a grand total of two. He was on fire.

"And you'll have to meet in the girls' bathroom," he added.

Never mind. He was an idiot.

"What do you mean, the girls' bathroom?" I demanded. "Why would I want to meet Justin Case in the girls' bathroom?"

"Because you're supposed to be Fiona Friend," he explained slowly, "and that's a *girl's* name."

Norris grinned. He was right again and he was really loving it.

That's why I stole his peanut butter.

 Saturday, November 9th

Cooking is not fun.

I told Mom I was doing a special survival project and had to fend for myself all weekend.

I'm not sure I'm going to make it.

My spaghetti looked like I dropped one of my wigs in a big cow pie and then repeatedly stomped on it. It didn't taste much better.

Mom keeps offering me cookies. Mr. Jones gave everyone a box of them at the parents' meeting. The smell's driving me crazy, but if I eat one of them, I become one of *them*. It's like having a whole field of bubble wrap in front of you and being told you can't walk on it.

I've been trying to take my mind off the cookies and the fact that I have to go into the girls' bathroom on Monday by doing some research on the internet. I need some help with the survival guide.

There were millions of pictures of "aliens," but none of them wore brown suits. I put in "evil alien teacher," but that just brought up a bunch of stuff about teachers giving too much homework. Then I put in "Can anyone help me defeat an alien principal who is hypnotizing everyone with candy and cookies?"

There are some very strange people out there.

I made an important editorial decision about the guide, though. I need a new pen name for it. I think Kenny Killzone should set the tone nicely.

Sunday, November 10th

I had a dream last night.

Well, not so much a dream as a stomach-churning nightmare that made me wake up screaming, "No! No! No! Not the monster cookies!" at the top of my lungs.

I was in the girls' bathroom. There were pictures of pink cows all over the walls and the carpet was made out of furry pencil cases. I was strapped down in a dentist's chair. Mr. Jones was leaning over me, dangling cookies into my mouth with a pair of tweezers.

Out of the corner of my eye, I could just make out his assistant. It was Norris. Well, it was Norris's head, arms, and legs sticking out of a huge jar of peanut butter.

I'm never going to sleep again.

What made it worse was when my parents rushed in to see what was the matter. They'd just about managed to get me to calm down when Mom said she'd get me some milk and *cookies*.

After that, I'm not sure that the neighbors got much sleep either.

On the plus side, my cooking's getting better. I managed to open a can of baked beans without injuring myself. And after I'd scraped off all the burned parts, my hot dog wasn't too shabby.

Next time Dad says he's going to take the batteries out of the smoke alarm *before* I start.

Monday, November 11th
Veterans Day
Thinking of you, Grandpa.

Mr. Jones has a big idea. He told us about it today in an assembly.

He glided in with a big black academic gown on. The rest of the staff followed behind him wearing the same gowns and the same smiles.

Mr. Jones got right to the point.

"Next week, Woodford School will have two days of Total School. This is one of my pioneering teaching techniques. I've been using it for twenty-three of your Earth years. The way it works is that for forty-eight Earth hours, everyone comes to school: students, teachers, and parents. And, for those forty-eight hours, no one goes home!

"We will learn together and live together for two whole days with no interference at all from the outside world."

Mr. Jones's eyes glinted. He had the look of a big purple hunter about to go on a hunting safari.

I felt like something about to get shot.

Mr. Jones continued, "As a result, your classes for this week will see a few minor changes. Cooking classes will be mandatory, as will first aid and lectures in personal hygiene. The week will end with a giant feast, and I have asked Ms. Briars to accelerate her rehearsal schedule for the school play so that it will be ready to perform on our final night together."

Ms. Briars looked delighted. But so did everybody else.

Permanently.

My cheek muscles were burning with the effort of smiling, but Mr. Jones wasn't quite finished yet. He dropped his voice so that it was almost a whisper.

"And just in case a certain journalist is thinking about contacting the press about my plans, he might like to know that I've done it already. If he wants, I can show him the headlines in my office. They're pretty good, if I do say so myself."

What is it with principals taking my headlines?

Mr. Jones spun on his heel and left with his gown swirling impressively behind him. He'd been practicing.

So it wasn't a great start to the week. And it was about to get worse.

It was time to go to the girls' bathroom.

The plan was to march in and get it over with as quick as possible. The plan was good and was going just fine.

Right up until Norris and me got to the door.

At which point, something deep within both of us screamed, "NOOOOOO!" at the top of its lungs.

I told myself I was a fearless undercover reporter. I told myself I'd been in situations far more dangerous than this. Then I took a long, slow breath and put my trembling hand on the door. I stamped on Norris's foot and then he put his hand on the door too.

Together we pushed and entered a world no boy was ever meant to see.

We were alone. I resisted the urge to punch the air and shout, "Yes!" Instead we ran straight into a stall and locked the door. I sat on the toilet seat, Norris sat on the tank.

Then we waited. Waited and hoped. Really, really hoped, that the next person to come in would be Justin Case and not a girl actually needing to use the bathroom.

Finally, we heard the door open.

Footsteps came our way. The person was in a rush, walking quickly and breathing heavily. They pulled open the stall door next to ours and fumbled with the lock. It was either Justin Case or someone desperate for a bathroom break.

There was a terrible silence. Any second I expected to hear a splash.

Eventually a weird, nervous voice said, "Hello."

I could have jumped for joy.

"Hi," I replied, trying really hard to sound like a girl. I think I tried too hard. When the echo died down there was more silence. I wasn't surprised.

"How are you?" I tried again, at about half the decibels.

"Good," replied the weird voice. "Thanks," it added after a bit.

Well, this conversation wasn't going well. There was more awkward silence. Then Norris farted.

That got things started.

"Hey! What's going on? I thought we were coming here to talk!"

"It wasn't me," I said, glaring at Norris, who had turned an interesting shade of pink.

"What do you mean, it wasn't you? I just heard you."

"It was my assistant."

"Assistant?!" Justin Case's voice was getting higher and higher.

"Yes."

"You have an assistant to go to the bathroom with you?"

"My assistant on the paper."

"You have an assistant for the toilet paper?! What kind of freak are you?"

"No! Not the toilet paper. What do you think I am? The *paper*. You know . . ."

"Oh, *that* paper."

Justin Case calmed down a little. I went back to glaring at Norris.

"Yes, that paper."

"So who are you?"

"I can't tell you."

"Why not?"

"Because if we don't know who the other person is, then we can't rat them out if we get caught."

Justin Case thought about this for a moment. "Okay, but why did they have to fart?"

"I don't know, that's a very good question," I said, still giving Norris the evil eye. "I'll ask her. Why did you have to fart?"

Norris shook his head. The other day, when he was

making all those points, I couldn't get him to stop talking. Now, all of a sudden, he'd clammed up. I wasn't going to let him off that easily.

"I'm sorry, I don't think Justin Case heard that!"

Norris's eyes widened in fear. He was going to have to try and speak like a girl.

"I'm sorry," he said, in a voice that threatened to crack the mirrors above the sinks. "I just ate a whole can of baked beans. I lost control. Sorry." The sweat was pouring off him now.

"It's all right," Justin Case said after a long pause. "I know what it's like. All I've eaten today are Oreos. Let's just get down to business. What are we going to do?"

"We need to find out what Mr. Jones is up to," I replied. "I don't like this Total School thing one bit."

"Me neither."

"Problem is, I've already followed him a bunch. He's bound to put two and two together if I bump into him again. You'll need to do it for a while."

"All right, I'll follow him," agreed Justin Case. "But you'll have to try and talk to Ms. Briars."

"Why would I want to do that?"

"Because she's the only other person who's not been affected."

"But I just saw her looking totally spaced out in the assembly, just like the rest of them."

"She always looks like that."

Justin Case had a point, but he could tell I wasn't convinced.

"She's a really picky eater. Only eats organic barley and vitamin pills and weird stuff, so Mr. Jones hasn't managed to get her to eat anything. We need everyone we can get."

"I guess," I said reluctantly. I'd rather talk to a brick

wall than Ms. Briars, but these were desperate times. "But what should I talk to her about? I mean, if she's not under his control, why isn't she doing something about him already?"

"She hasn't done anything about it because she hasn't noticed."

"Hasn't noticed! Hasn't noticed that the rest of the school has been turned into zombies? How can she not notice?"

"Because she's Ms. Briars! Look, we have to let her know. No one's going to take us seriously, but maybe they'll listen to an adult, even if it is Ms. Briars."

I sighed. "Fine. But how do I get her attention?"

Justin Case didn't give me an answer right away. I got the feeling it was because I wasn't going to like it.

"You'll have to audition for the play," he whispered.

Justin Case was right.

Mr. Jones lied to us. I saw the Total School headlines at a newsstand on my way into school. They're total garbage.

"TOTAL SCHOOL" PLAN TO IMPROVE ATTITUDES AMONG STUDENTS AND PARENTS AT WOODFORD SCHOOL

Yawn.

NO ONE'S TOO COOL FOR "TOTAL SCHOOL"

Trying way too hard.

MR. JONES READY TO TEACH US MORE LESSONS

Oh, please.

I know a bedpost that could do better than that.

I also discovered, beyond all possible doubt, that Ms. Briars is totally bonkers.

In fact, I don't feel I'm getting the high standard of education that I deserve.

I auditioned for the school play, as agreed. The posters said it was going to be *Macbeth*. When I got down to the drama studio, I found out I was the only one who had turned up. So now Ms. Briars wants me to play Macbeth. She's going to play Lady Macbeth. I said what about all the other characters. She said she'd play them as well.

If I don't get horribly murdered by Mr. Jones before next Friday, it looks like I'm going to die of embarrassment on stage instead.

I think Ms. Briars told me a bit about the story, but I tuned out after a couple of minutes. The studio is a weird room. It messes with your head.

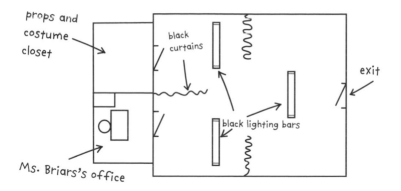

It's about the size of two normal classrooms with four black walls and three black doors.

One leads to Ms. Briars's office, one to the props and costume closet, and one to the exit. On the ceiling are three black lighting bars with black lights on them and some black curtains to divide the room up.

I'm guessing Ms. Briars likes black.

When she'd finished talking about *Macbeth*, I tried to bring the conversation around to the fact that the school has been taken over by a psychotic alien. Ms. Briars said she valued my imagination but that I needed to channel it into my character. I tried again and asked her if she'd noticed anything strange about the school recently. She thought about it and said that yes, now that I mentioned it, she hadn't had anyone actually turn up for auditions before.

I'm supposed to learn my lines by tomorrow. There's only about three thousand of them.

 **Wednesday, November 13th**
World Kindness Day
But apparently we still have to go to school.

We had a Home Economics class this morning.

That means cooking.

Mr. Frazer told us we'd be making hamburgers. He hauled in three large sacks and said they were full of all the finest ingredients we'd ever need. I thought they smelled like sweaty socks, but everyone else thought they smelled great.

We were split into pairs, given a recipe, and told to get

on with it. Basically it involved putting a big spoonful from each sack into a bowl, adding some water, and mixing it all up until it made a big gray blob. Then we took the big gray blob out, cut it into circles, and fried it.

After that it smelled like fried sweaty socks.

To finish it off, we sliced open a bun, buttered it, and stuck the "burger" in. I'd be lying if I said it looked like a hamburger. It looked like a big, gray blob in a bun. Mr. Frazer told us to eat them. Luckily I was with Lucy Hutch so I let her eat mine too.

Norris set up another meeting with Justin Case after lunch. There was good and bad news.

The good news was that Justin Case said this time it was only fair to have it in the boys' bathroom.

Justin Case said he'd been trying to keep track of Mr. Jones, but it was impossible. He said it was like he was everywhere. He said that, one time, he'd seen Mr. Jones turn a corner at the end of one hall and ten seconds later, he'd come walking up behind him from the other direction. I made a note of it for the alien survival guide.

And then there was the bad news.

Sally Coyle has missed two days of school.

Sally Coyle never misses school. She lives for it.

She's the kind of traitor who reminds the teacher to collect an assignment that's due. The kind of robot who signs up for every single extracurricular activity possible. And the kind of person whose pencil case is better equipped than the average fire station.

The only thing that could keep Sally Coyle away from school is the kind of disease that needs a bunch of people in hazmat suits to stop it from wiping out all of the civilian population.

Justin Case said he'd try and get to the bottom of it.

I'm not sure he's going to like what he finds when he gets there.

Then it was my turn to tell Justin Case about Ms. Briars. I told him she was a dangerous lunatic who shouldn't be left in charge of a glass of water, let alone a school play. I told him she had no idea what Mr. Jones was up to and that trying to talk to her would be like trying to talk to a rock.

Justin Case said I had to give it another try.

Then we talked about the hamburgers. Justin Case bets they're not just for mind control. He doesn't know what else they're for, but he doesn't like them. Norris thought they looked quite tempting.

That's because all he's eaten this week are pickles.

We agreed to meet again tomorrow back in the girls' bathroom.

Whoopee.

Thursday, November 14th

World Diabetes Day

Well, that's ironic.

It didn't take very long to figure out what the hamburgers do.

I don't know what's in them, and I don't want to know what's in them, but I do know that the whole school is now fat. Yesterday, Goran Sarta was a skinny sixth grader. Today, he looks like Mr. Potato Head.

Before

After

And it's only going to get a whole lot worse. We got new class schedules today. I don't know why they bothered printing them off. It's really easy to remember:

	Thursday
9 a.m. - 10 a.m.	Cooking I
10 a.m. - 12 p.m.	Cooking II
1 p.m. - 4 p.m.	Cooking III

You know what? I don't think Mr. Jones wants to take over our minds.

I think Mr. Jones wants to eat us.

The hamburgers don't just make you fat. They have another side effect.

Gas. Both ends.

Walking from one classroom to another has become a major challenge. First, you have to negotiate the fat, wobbly zombies themselves. Then you have to negotiate the gas cloud they move around in. I've walked into at least two doorways already and was choking so much at one point that I nearly fell into the trash can outside of the art room.

It would be great material for the paper.

If it wasn't for the fact that we're all going to die.

Norris and I brainstormed and came up with a plan to blend in and make us look as fat as the other kids. We filled some trash bags with scrunched-up paper, and we stuffed it all under our shirts. We rustle a bit when we move, but I don't think anyone's noticed.

The play rehearsal was the most embarrassing time of my life. We did the first part where Macbeth meets the witches. Ms. Briars said I had to look "murderous" and "confused" and "vulnerable" all at the same time while she pretended to be all the witches. There's a line in the play about the witches all having beards, so she looked in the costume closet and found herself a different colored beard for each witch.

If I don't get those images out of my head fast, I'll need some serious therapy when this is all over.

I was so traumatized I almost didn't notice some very important information.

Ms. Briars is armed to the teeth.

At the start of the play, Macbeth is supposed to be this super warrior dude. He comes in all caked in blood and fresh from the battlefield and stuff. So Ms. Briars got me a big shield and this gigantic sword to help me look the part. She said it was a genuine claymore. I asked why she had one. She said that she goes to lots of Renaissance fairs during the summer and that she has tons of old-fashioned weapons.

Result.

I told Norris and Justin Case about it later. I said that they should join the play and then we could form a little army. I'd like to see Mr. Jones offer me some of his candy with three feet of sharpened steel at his throat.

Justin Case was being really quiet. I asked him what he'd like to do to Mr. Jones with a claymore. That's when he started crying like a girl.

I don't mean that just because he was crying that he was acting like a girl. I mean he was crying and it sounded like an actual girl crying.

I thought I'd better give him a moment, but Norris isn't into moments.

"Why are you crying like a girl?" he asked.

"Oh, that's so typical," Justin Case wailed in between sobs. "You think that just because I start crying I sound like a girl."

"No, it's not that," Norris replied. "It's your voice. You sound like a girl."

"So do you, a little bit."

"That's because I *am* a girl." Norris said, raising the pitch of his voice as far as it would go.

"Oh, please!" Justin Case snapped. "If you're a girl, then I'm Beyoncé! That's the worst impression of a girl I've ever heard. You sound like an elephant that's been sucking a helium balloon. And as for you, 'Fiona Friend,'" Justin Case continued, half crying, half shouting, "don't think you're any better. I knew you were a boy before I even heard you!"

"How come?" I squealed — because I was still pretending to be a girl. Obviously.

"Oh, come on! *The Woodford Word*! It's all one big ego trip. We're running out of time here so let's stop messing around, all right? I'm a girl and you're obviously boys. I mean, only boys could write notes that were so arrogant!"

"Well, only girls could whine so much!" I yelled back.

"Well, only boys could be so rude!"

"Well, only girls have to use three exclamation marks!

And, anyway, if I'm such a bighead, why have you been so desperate to get my attention?"

"Because we need to stop him."

Justin Case was starting to calm herself down again. Our deep and meaningful discussion had obviously helped clear the air. She blew her nose.

"So get over yourself and listen," Justin Case began, using her own voice clearly for the first time. I suppose it was kind of a nice voice. "He has Sally, I'm sure of it. I was outside the principal's office and found a bit of paper scrunched up on the floor. It was ripped out of Sally's planner. It said, 'Help me.'"

I let Justin Case's words sink in. It was almost impossible to believe.

"Sally Coyle ripped a page out of her planner?" I asked.

"It's worse than that," Justin Case wailed. "The handwriting was awful!"

Justin Case started sobbing again. I didn't blame her.

I wasn't super happy about letting a second person know who Jonny Jakes really was, especially since that person had turned out to be a girl, but it looked like I didn't have any other option. Our future was looking horribly bleak. By the end of next week, Mr. Jones was going to eat all of us. And, if we didn't do anything about it, Sally Coyle was about to become the appetizer.

"Look," I explained, after Justin Case had blown her nose for the millionth time, "I don't want to know who you are and I certainly don't want you to know who I am, but, if we're going to rescue Sally, I guess we don't have a choice."

"I won't tell anyone," Justin Case promised.

"You better not."

"Cross my heart and h—"

"Don't bother."

"But —"

"Like you said, we need to get real, so let's just get on with it, okay? I'll stand up on my toilet and then you stand up on yours."

"What about the other guy?" Justin Case asked, meaning Norris.

"If he stands up on the toilet, he'll break it."

"Hey!" protested Norris.

"Oh, be quiet! Right, let's just get this over with."

"Okay, then."

"No stupid girly screaming?"

"No screaming."

"You promise?"

"I promise."

"Okay, then."

Slowly, we both stood up.

Justin Case shrieked. "Oh my god, it's —"

"What did I say about the screaming! Why not just write my name on a piece of paper and give it to Mr. Jones?"

"Sorry, I didn't mean to," she apologized. "I won't do it again. Okay?"

"Okay. Just make sure you don't."

"Who is she?" Norris asked, feeling a little left out.

"It's just Julie Singh!" I shouted back down.

I can't remember exactly what Julie Singh said after that. Whatever it was, it was loud.

Mrs. Singh,
secretary/foghorn

Julie Singh,
her daughter;
overly sensitive

Friday, November 15th

It's just past midnight. Operation Midnight Rescue is about to begin. Justin Case has just confirmed we're good to go, and now I'm waiting for a call from Black Panther (Norris said he wanted a code name too).

If I don't get back, this will be the end of my journal. The annoying thing is I know I'll come up with a much better last line than that in about ten minutes.

It's three a.m.

Operation Midnight Rescue was a success. Target identified and secured. Bogeys neutralized.

I'm not sure what that last part means. I just like saying it.

Five minutes before midnight, we each crept out of our houses. We were wearing black pants and black sweaters, and Julie had given us tights to put over our faces. It sounds wrong but it looked right.

We met in the bushes by the school gate right at midnight. It was pitch black. We couldn't see a thing. Then Norris said maybe we should take the tights off until we got out of the bushes.

When we were sure no one was around, we rolled under the main gate and ran across the yard. At the front door, Julie got out the keys she'd stolen from her mom's purse. There are some advantages to having the daughter of the principal's secretary join your investigation.

I shone my flashlight at the door. As Julie slipped the key in the lock, I could see the alarm code written on the back of her hand.

Julie looked at us. Once she'd opened the door, there was no turning back.

We nodded and she turned the key.

The alarm started beeping. Julie opened the door and rushed inside.

That was the worst part. Waiting for Julie to punch in the code with that horrible beeping sound getting faster and faster. I was sure somebody was going to hear it. I kept expecting police sirens to start wailing at any moment.

Then, finally, the beeping stopped.

We were in.

We tiptoed carefully along the hall, keeping our flashlights trained on the floor so that we moved along in three tiny pools of light. Without anybody in it, the school didn't feel like a school at all. It felt like we were walking around inside the belly of some giant, sleeping beast.

As we got close to Mr. Jones's office, we slowed down to a crawl, pausing between every step to listen. It was deathly quiet. I half wished Mr. Jones would just jump out and get it over with.

Julie gestured at Norris to look through the keyhole. He bent down and put his eye to the door.

"Anything?" I whispered.

He stood up and shook his head.

Julie took hold of the door handle and twisted it as gently as she could. When it was fully turned, she pushed.

Nothing happened. The door was locked. Mr. Jones obviously took his security a little more seriously than Mr. Hardy had.

Julie brought out the bunch of keys again. Her hands were shaking and the keys started to jangle. Each little clink sounded like a cymbal crash in the deserted hallway. I held on to her wrist and the shaking died down.

Eventually she found the right one and turned it in the keyhole. The door creaked open slowly.

Mr. Jones's office was empty. Or at least it was empty

of Mr. Jones, which was the main thing. We took the tights off our heads again and let out a long sigh.

We still didn't feel like speaking, so we silently ran our flashlights over the room. It was unnaturally tidy. No documents marked "Top Secret Plans for Taking Over the World" left out on the desk, no alien gadgets lying around, and no sign whatsoever of Sally Coyle.

I was beginning to think that we'd wasted our time when I noticed my light reflect off a dent in the steel storage cabinet. It wasn't much, but in a room that was otherwise perfect, it stood out.

I nudged Julie and flicked my light over the spot. We walked over. I started tapping the outside of the cabinet and listening to the sound it made. I don't know why. It just felt like the something I should do.

Unsurprisingly, it sounded like a steel cabinet.

Until it tapped back.

I tapped again. The cabinet did the same. Then it whispered, "Don't scream!" in a terrified voice.

"Why not?" I asked it.

"Don't scream!" it said again.

"I wasn't going to!" I replied, a little annoyed at getting lectured by a piece of furniture.

"Okay, sure, we promise we won't scream," Julie whispered, nudging me out of the way and giving me a dirty look. "Is that you, Sally? We're here to rescue you."

"Yes, it's me," Sally whispered through the cabinet door. "Thank you so much for coming. Look, I'm sorry I keep saying it, but you really can't scream. Put your hands over your mouths. Please."

Julie motioned at us to cover our mouths.

"Okay, Sally, we're doing it," Julie assured her. "We won't scream, I promise. What do you want us to do next?"

"Do you have your hands over your mouths?"

"Yethhh," Julie mumbled through her fingers. "Whath shuth we du nxt?"

"Okay, now you need to look up."

We all looked up. We all screamed.

Luckily, it sounded more like three goldfish celebrating a touchdown.

Four feet above our heads were two gigantic vampire bats. They were enormous and were twirling upside down from the ceiling, fast asleep in their folded black wings.

But they weren't wings; they were academic gowns. And they weren't bats. They were Mr. Jones.

There were two of him.

"Can you see them?" Sally asked.

"Yeth," we replied.

"Okay, you can take your hands away now. Disgusting, isn't it?"

I disagreed with Sally Coyle about many things, but this wasn't one of them. Mr. Jones was weird enough without sleeping like a bat. To make it worse, gravity was pulling his features toward the floor. His stomach was sagging down to his chin and his massive nose was swinging below his head.

"I didn't think anyone would come," she continued. "I'm so grateful. You'll need to get the keys to open the cabinet; they're clipped on to his belt."

"Which one?" I whispered back.

"The belt around his waist, silly."

"No, he means which him is the right him?" Julie asked.

"Oh, right. It took me a little while to tell them apart. He's the one with the slightly bigger nose."

We looked up. Sure enough, the Mr. Jones on the left did have a slightly bigger nose, and we could just make out the silver tops of a set of keys under his robe. I carefully moved a chair underneath him and got up on it.

"Who's the other one?" Norris wanted to know while I tried to figure out how I was going to unclip the keys. It didn't help that Mr. Jones kept spinning all the time.

"That's Mrs. Jones," Sally replied, just as I was about to make a grab for the keys.

"Euuurrghhhh! That's gross!" Norris retched.

"I know, and when they kiss they make this sort of —"

"Too much information!" I whispered as loudly as I dared.

It was too loud. Mr. Jones shuffled in his strange bed.

We waited, completely frozen, until he seemed to settle back to sleep. Pointedly, I put my finger on my lips and glared at Norris.

The keys swung back into range. I held my breath and reached up.

I'd nearly gotten the keys clear of the belt when Mr. Jones began to spin back the other way again. As I pulled the keys off, the clip caught very slightly on his belt loop. It wasn't much, but it switched the direction of his spin.

Mr. Jones's breathing changed and became shallower. We had to move. Fast. I passed the keys to Norris.

"Which one?" he asked.

"It's a small one. I think it was gold," Sally whispered. "I can't really remember. You'll just have to try them."

As quick as he could, Norris started trying out the keys. He wasn't quick enough. Mr. Jones was waking up and so was his wife. They started mumbling and doing all those weird things you do just before you wake up.

"Come on!" I urged.

"I'm trying!" Norris moaned. "Wait, I don't think I tried this one yet . . . yes!"

Sure enough, the steel door swung open and there, tightly coiled, was Sally Coyle.

"Quick, let's run," I said, hardly bothering to whisper anymore. The Joneses' mumbling was getting less mumbly all the time.

"We can't," Julie answered. "Look at her. She's been in there for hours. She can barely move."

It was true; Sally was moving like someone coming out of a deep freeze.

Norris sprang to the rescue. He bent down and got his hands underneath Sally's knees and shoulders. Just as he'd scooped her up, a voice above us rang out.

"Who's there? What's going on? Brian? Is that you?"

Mrs. Jones was rubbing her eyes.

"Brian! Someone's here. What did I tell you about locking doors?"

"I did lock it!" Mr. Jones replied groggily. "What's going on?"

But before they had a chance to find out, we had scrambled out the door. I was halfway down the hall when I realized Julie wasn't with us. I looked back to see her fiddling with the key in the lock.

"What are you doing?" I hissed.

"Locking the door," she hissed back. As soon she'd done it, she snapped the key in the lock and ran after us.

"That should give us a little more time."

We didn't bother closing the front door as we all flew across the playground. Norris was carrying Sally under his arm like a giant football. For once in her life, Sally couldn't get out of school fast enough.

It was too dangerous for Sally to stay with Julie, so me and Norris had to fight over who didn't want her more.

She's at my house.

She's hiding under my bed. She keeps moaning that she's fed up with being curled up in dark, unpleasant places. I keep telling her to be quiet and to be grateful that at least I'm not going to eat her.

I gave her some of my math homework to keep her happy.

Back at school, Mr. Jones has gone ballistic; anyone would think he'd had a bad night's sleep. In fact, the smiles have been wearing off everyone since they stopped eating candy and started eating hamburgers.

They're still under some sort of spell, but now they've stopped looking so happy about it.

As well as ripping open everyone's lockers, Mr. Jones now has student bodyguards. He doesn't go anywhere without ten giant hench-kids around him. He's after me big time.

And if he figures out who I am, he's going to suck my brains out my ear with a straw.

He spent the whole morning going into classrooms and putting kids into trances, trying to catch me.

We were just at the eating stage of our cooking class when he came into our room. He'd been working through the school methodically, from class to class, so I knew what was coming.

He put everyone in a trance right away, including his bodyguards, and started wandering among us, sniffing and poking.

He'd almost gotten to me when I realized that, although

the stuffed trash bags under my pants and shirt were doing their job, my face was nowhere near as fat as it should be. I took a deep breath and puffed up my cheeks as far out as they would go.

Have you ever tried puffing up your cheeks for more than ten seconds?

I wouldn't recommend it.

When he eventually came to me, I was doing my best to look like I was in a trance, but I could feel myself growing redder and redder. The blood was pounding in my head and a bead of sweat began to trickle down my cheek. As he leaned toward me, spots of light started jumping around in front of my eyes and I could feel myself swaying. I was about to pass out when something terrible happened.

It came from Barry Devine's pants.

It smelled like a vat of stale vomit and came with a rasp like the sound of splitting pants.

There was a reason for that.

Mr. Jones sniffed and turned his head. A purple cloud was puffing out of Barry's mangled pants. Mr. Jones smiled.

He made his way across the room to take a closer look and I finally got to breathe. Barry Devine had been pretty fat before the hamburgers came along; now he was a boy mountain. Mr. Jones looked at his triple chin with satisfaction and prodded him like a piece of meat at the butcher's. Then Mr. Jones whistled.

In a few seconds, a large shadow fell across the doorway. Mrs. Jones had arrived.

She came over to her husband and they began to do this weird circling thing around Barry Devine. They sort of dipped and raised their heads at each other as they went round and round. It reminded me of a pair of swans from a film we'd seen in biology about the courtship behavior of birds.

Well, aside from the fact they didn't look anything like swans.

The circling got quicker and quicker and the head bobbing got more and more extreme. When it felt like they couldn't go any faster, the Joneses stopped. Their backs were arched, their necks stretched out, and their chins pointed straight up at the ceiling.

They stayed like that for several seconds, like toys whose batteries had suddenly run out. Then slowly they began to relax. Their necks went back to their original position, their chins drew back in, and together they left the room.

The kids' trances lifted gradually.

Unfortunately, the fart cloud decided to stick around.

Even by the school's new standards of foul and unpleasant smells, this one was something else. It lingered under the counters, it swirled above the sinks, and it swam right up our nostrils.

For the first time, I wasn't the only one who was laying off the hamburgers.

At lunchtime, me, Norris, and Julie showed up for *Macbeth* rehearsals. Ms. Briars almost melted with excitement.

"A cast!" she squealed with delight. "A whole cast! You don't know how long I've dreamed of a day like this! Don't go!" she pleaded as Norris decided that he didn't like having a teacher hold his hands and try to dance with him.

"I have an idea for the start of the play, Ms. Briars," I said quickly, before Norris could get to the door. "How about we do this big ol' battle scene, to show what Macbeth's been doing before he meets the witches?

We could all do a slow motion fight — you know, swinging our swords around our heads and stuff."

Ms. Briars shut her eyes and tried to imagine what it would look like.

"Yes, yes. I can see it," she said, swaying about. "Macbeth appears through the mist, his sword flashing in the spotlight. Alongside him, his trusty comrade, Banquo, bludgeoning the foe with each mighty swoop of his mace . . ."

"Yeah! And Macbeth could actually have two swords, sort of like a double lightsaber," I added.

"And I could be Macbeth's servant with a catapult and a dagger," Julie suggested.

"And Banky-what's-his-name could have a big spear," Norris joined in, suddenly much more interested in theater than he had been a minute ago. "And a big shield."

Between us, we got her up to four swords, three shields, two spears, a mace, a dagger, a catapult, and a pikestaff (whatever that was) before we thought we might be pushing it too far. We even managed to persuade her to let us take some of it home to practice with over the weekend.

If the school board ever gets wind of this, Ms. Briars is going to be in big trouble.

Saturday, November 16th
Inventor of the gas mask died, 1966
We could so use him right now.

Norris and Julie sneaked around this morning so we could all get the full story from Sally. We moved my bed against the door so my parents wouldn't be able to come in and surprise us.

Sally told us a lot of what we already knew: the trances, the candy, the hamburgers. We asked her why she had been taken. She said that Mr. Jones thought she had something to do with *The Woodford Word* because she was always writing stuff down. She said he searched all through her bag, but realized she was telling the truth when he saw that she was the only student he'd ever met who actually did the practice problems in the back of the textbooks without being told to.

She told us more about Mrs. Jones. Apparently she's been here the whole time. That's why Julie had such a hard time following Mr. Jones; half the time she'd been following his wife.

Norris asked what she thought they were going to do with her. Sally wasn't sure but said they kept pouring this disgusting oil over her and tried to get her to eat some hamburgers. She refused to do it because studies have revealed that eating too much saturated fat reduces brain activity.

Unfortunately, Sally hadn't figured out the whole we're-going-to-get-eaten thing until Norris pointed it out.

Next time he tries to break bad news to someone, I'm going to have to insist on a two-minute warning.

Spent the afternoon on the survival guide. I have the front page down:

And it's going to start with a few basic dos and don'ts.

1. <u>Don't</u> EVER accept food from an alien. It is their principal weapon. The food will either
   a) mess with your mind
   b) turn you into a blob
   or probably c) do both.

2. <u>Do</u> be on your guard at all times. They might be smart, they might even seem nice, but remember, they just want to eat you.

3. <u>Don't</u> let the fact that they don't have teeth fool you. As far as I can tell, they have at least two sets of lips, three tongues, and saliva that could break down a horse (if in doubt, see 2).

4. <u>Do</u> carry a barf bag with you at all times.
   Whether it's their ability to suddenly rearrange
   their body mass so that certain parts bulge
   out unexpectedly, or the smell they
   make their victims produce, the fact
   is, sooner or later, they're going to
   make you puke.

Sunday, November 17th
Dad's birthday
Oops.

Just when I thought I never wanted to go back to school
again, my parents insisted on some "quality family
time." I tried to protest but then my dad brought up the
"you didn't even bother to buy me a card" thing and
guilt-tripped me into it.

So we're going to spend his WHOLE birthday together.

Suddenly the thought of being eaten alive by Mr. Jones
doesn't seem so bad.

My parents are really excited about Total School. Apparently their school days were the best days of their lives.

I hate to think how bad their jobs are.

For some reason, Mr. Jones wants the parents to be wearing school uniforms when they come to Total School, so we went into town on the world's worst shopping trip. Everywhere you looked, fat children watched in horror as their parents tried to squeeze into white shirts, gray pants, and green sweaters.

If that wasn't bad enough, the uniform seemed to magically turn them all into misbehaving school children. Now I know why all my dad's hair fell out. If I had to tell them once that escalators should be treated with respect, I had to tell them a hundred times.

When we got back home, it turned out the torture was only just beginning. They told me I had to pretend to be a teacher and teach them some of the stuff I've been learning this year. I told them it would go way over their heads. They said bring it on. So I talked about plate tectonics, square roots, and sonnets.

I was right.

Worst of all, I had to watch them dance to the *Greatest Hits of the '80s* album they'd gotten. If there's a more terrible form of torture known to mankind than seeing your dad play air guitar on the couch while your mom pretends to sing into a hairbrush, I don't want to know about it.

Eventually I was allowed to go to my room.

Sally was trying to log on to my laptop.

"Hey! Get off! That's private!" I yelled.

"I wasn't doing anything," she whined. "I was bored. You can't expect me to just lie under your bed all day."

"You have it easy. I just had to spend the whole day with my parents, pretending to be back at school."

Sally burst into tears.

It turns out that would have been her perfect day.

Luckily it wasn't too long before Norris and Julie stopped by for a meeting.

"Why are your mom and dad laughing so much?" Norris asked.

I sighed. "I haven't managed to get a word of sense out of them all day. I'm not sure Mr. Jones knows what he's getting himself into."

"What I don't get," Julie said, "is why, if he's planning to eat us, does he want our moms and dads there to watch?"

"Maybe he's planning on eating them too," I said hopefully.

That started Sally crying again.

"I was joking."

"It's not very funny!" Sally wailed.

"I think we have to make our move as soon as possible," Julie cut in, patting Sally on the back and trying to change the subject. "The longer Mr. Jones stays in charge, the stronger he'll get."

"Sounds good," Norris agreed.

"Oh, sure, it's a great plan," I said. "Just remind me how we get Mr. and Mrs. Jones in the same place at the same time, avoid being pulverized by their new bodyguards, and create a big enough diversion so that we can catch them all by surprise?"

Julie told me to shut up if I couldn't be more constructive.

I told her to shut up if she couldn't stop being so stupid.

Then Norris decided to join in.

"Stop it! Just stop it!" Sally screamed.

We all stopped and stared at her. She had the pikestaff in her hand and was waving it around dangerously.

"I'm warning you!" Sally yelled, pointing the pointy part of the pikestaff at each of us in turn. Her eyes were wild. "I know nobody likes me! I know everyone thinks I'm just a goody-two-shoes teacher's pet! But I've had enough! I may be a nerd, but I'm a nerd on the edge!"

"It's okay, Sally," Julie said, putting her hands up. "We don't think you're just a big nerd at all, do we, guys?"

Me and Norris shook our heads.

"Um, no, of course not. We think you're uh . . . you uh . . .

just have a giant brain," I said, hoping I'd gotten out the right words in the right order. "Don't we, Norris?"

"That's right, we think you're great," Norris said encouragingly.

It would have looked better if he wasn't still shaking his head.

Luckily, Sally was starting to calm down.

"Arguing isn't going to get us anywhere," she said, and this time I made sure our heads were all doing the right thing.

"Let's just keep thinking about it," Julie agreed, carefully easing the pikestaff out of Sally's hands. "We have another rehearsal tomorrow during lunch. Maybe we'll have thought of something by then."

It's nearly midnight. I'm still thinking.

Monday, November 18th

Thinking hurts. I'm trying a different approach.

I'm working on my alien survival guide and hoping I can give myself the answer by not trying to think about it too much — although it's two a.m., I haven't eaten all day, and there's a chance that I'm so tired that I'm making no sense whatsoever.

Strengths:

drool

1. Five hearts. Hard to stop all of them at the same time.

2. Five eyes that can move around their faces, giving them pretty much 360-degree vision.

3. They're annoyingly smart.

4. They've figured out how to control people's minds using food.

5. Mmmm food.

6. I want some chips.

Weaknesses:

This part hasn't been going so well.

Got it!!!

Julie was right. The longer we wait, the stronger Mr. Jones gets. Everything's going his way and it's only a matter of time before he crushes us in his evil grasp.

I went back to racking my brain, trying to think of something that would give us an edge. So there are two of them. So they've got a whole bunch of bodyguards. So everyone is under their control. But Mr. Jones has to have at least one weakness.

Then I finally realized what it was.

Mr. Jones has never seen *Ninja Force 2*.

Specifically, he hasn't seen the part where Ninja Force takes out the two evil Japanese warlords who have been holding the humble village of Fudai at ransom.

It's so simple.

All we have to do is: get a hold of some minor explosives; devise a plan for getting Mr. and Mrs. Jones into two narrow gorges at the same time (hallways will also work); divide ourselves into pairs for a synchronized double ambush; and perfect the Leap of the Double-Backed Tiger before dispatching the enemy with the razor-sharp weapons we're whirling above our heads. By the time we're done, Mr. and Mrs. Jones will have more holes in them than cartoon cheese.

It's going to be awesome. I can't wait to tell the others.

I wish it wasn't four in the morning.

I'd gotten about three seconds of sleep when Mom shook me by the shoulder and told me I was late for school.

I said I'd only just gone to sleep.

She said it was 8:30 and pulled my covers off.

She's like that on Mondays.

School was really weird in the morning. There were no special assemblies, no patrols, no inspections, and, best of all, no cooking classes. It was like a normal day again. The teachers were normal too. I actually laughed at one of Mr. King's jokes. It wasn't funny — it just felt good to be so bored again.

"Something's up," Julie said the moment we got to the drama studio.

"Yeah, but what?" I asked.

"I don't know, but I don't like it. Did you notice how quiet it's been? Oh, you can come out now, Sally," she said, unzipping the huge hockey bag she'd been dragging behind her. "Sorry about the socks, but I thought the smell would put off anyone who got suspicious."

Sally crawled out. She had her hand over her mouth and her nose was scrunched up. She wasn't having a good week.

I was just about to tell everyone my brilliant plan when Ms. Briars appeared.

"Places, everyone! Places!" she shrieked. "I want to try the second witches scene! Come along now, we have a lot to get through!"

It was time to break the bad news. I wasn't sure how she was going to take it, but I couldn't take much more of *Macbeth*.

"Um, Ms. Briars, there's something we really need to talk to you about."

"This is not the time for arguing over artistic differences! We've got a show to put on!"

"It's not about the play."

"But what could possibly be more important than the play?" Ms. Briars asked, genuinely shocked.

Norris decided it was time for some straight talk. He was good at it.

"Mr. Jones is an evil alien. We've got to stop him. He keeps putting everyone in a trance and he wants to eat us."

Ms. Briars opened her mouth to speak but shut it when she realized that, for once, she didn't have anything to say. She looked at us through her huge glasses as if she had only just seen us clearly for the first time. We all nodded.

She looked confused. She looked surprised. She looked like a drama teacher who'd just been told her boss was a dangerous, child-eating lunatic.

She ran her hands along her necklace and twiddled the beads, deep in thought. Then something seemed to click into place.

"That *would* explain a lot," she said.

"That's why we've been coming to the rehearsals," Julie said. "We wanted to tell an adult. Mr. Jones has tricked everyone else. They've all eaten some of his food. The candy messes with your head and the hamburgers turn you into a blob. You're the only one left."

"So you're not here for the smell of the greasepaint? The music of the bard doesn't sing to you?"

"Huh?" said Norris, who'd been enjoying all the straight talk.

"Oh, it's nothing. I just thought that perhaps . . ." Her voice trailed off as she walked absentmindedly to the props closet. She picked up one of the witches' wigs and spun it slowly on her fingers.

I was just starting to wonder if we should have broken the news to her more gently when she turned back to us. A new expression was on her face. Her eyes were sharp, her chin stuck out, and her lips were thin. She almost looked like a real teacher.

"Never mind! Never mind!" she yelled, her voice suddenly as hard and sharp as her face. "You're right! This is a call to arms! This is no time for strutting and fretting about our hour upon the stage. This is a time for action! We have things to do!"

She paused, her fist punching the air. "What exactly are we going to do, by the way?"

I smiled. "I'm glad you asked. Hands up, who's seen *Ninja Force 2*!"

Ten minutes later, we were ready to rehearse. Ms. Briars had turned off the smoke alarm and gotten some theatrical smoke bombs ready to set off. I had taught everyone the basics of the Leap of the Double-Backed Tiger. We were going to practice with sticks for swords and a speaker with a sheet over it to represent Mr. Jones.

The first run-through wasn't great. The smoke got us confused. The speaker survived, but it was a good thing we'd only used sticks, otherwise Sally would no longer have two ears.

By the third try, though, things were looking a lot better. We felt ready to try two attacks at the same time. Mrs. Jones was going to be a table flipped up on its end.

I was about to give the signal to start when the door to the studio opened.

"Ah, the theater kids," said an all-too-familiar voice. "I thought so."

Mr. Jones smiled at his wife as they squeezed into the studio along with their bodyguards. He wasn't handsome at the best of times, but being smug made him look even more ugly.

"I told you it was the one class we hadn't checked, dear. How nice to see you all here. Hello again, Sally. And well done, Ms. Briars!" Mr. Jones clapped his weird hands sarcastically. "I honestly didn't think you had it in you!"

Ms. Briars's chin stuck out another inch.

"I apologize for the interruption — I know how enthusiastic you are about the dramatic arts, but, as I'm sure you'll agree, there are some important issues we need to discuss. Oh, come now, please don't bother," he said as I made a half-hearted effort to pack some of the paper back under my shirt and pretend to go into a trance. "I think it's time to stop playing games now, don't you? Our little game is over. I won."

"In your dreams, fat face!" I yelled.

"Fat face? Is that the best you can do, Jonny Jakes?" Mr. Jones chuckled. The bodyguards copied him. "I thought you were supposed to be good with words."

"At least I don't have to brainwash everyone just to get a laugh, booger breath!"

My insults were getting worse. They were, however, distracting Mr. Jones from the fact that Ms. Briars was edging her way over to the pile of weapons.

"Very good." Mr. Jones clapped again. "Your parents must be very proud. How are they, by the way? Are they looking forward to coming back to school? I'm so looking forward to having them all here."

"You'll never get away with it!" I screamed.

It turns out that thinking you're about to die does nothing for your ability to say anything original.

Mr. Jones lapped it up. In fact, he was enjoying himself so much that he and Mrs. Jones had forgotten to stay behind their bodyguards. They'd wandered, unprotected, into the middle of the room. They'd also forgotten to keep an eye on what all their other prisoners were doing.

I looked at Norris. He was ready.

"Jonny, Jonny, I'm so disappointed in you," Mr. Jones crowed. Now Julie and Sally were ready. "Didn't you learn anything in English? If you're not careful, you'll be telling me that 'the game is up' and that I'd 'better come quietly if I know what's good for me.'"

Ms. Briars looked like she'd been born ready. It had to be here. It had to be now.

I'd always dreamed of executing the Leap of the Double-Backed Tiger.

It was time to live the dream.

I shouted the Ninja Force attack command.

"Ninja Force, ready! Ninja Force, go!"

The girls darted into position. Ms. Briars threw me my claymore and hit the detonator. The room exploded with smoke.

Norris and I ran onto the girls' backs as Julie and Sally sprung upward, growling and snarling at the same time. We somersaulted in perfect unison and plunged dramatically into the swirling smoke, our weapons ready for action as we screamed out the Ninja Force battle cry.

I can't believe no one took a picture.

When I landed, I was face-to-face with an astonished Mr. Jones. Victory was mine. I drew back the claymore and was about to thrust forward when Norris's face suddenly appeared in front of me.

He'd gotten disorientated and instead of thrusting at Mrs. Jones, he was thrusting at me. Somehow I managed to dodge the vicious point of Norris's pikestaff and parry the enormous wooden shaft with my claymore, but by then the face of Mr. Jones had vanished.

"Just get him!" I screamed, ignoring Norris's apology.

I spun, slicing through the smoke with my heavy blade. At the end of its arc, the sword hit something that felt kind of like a hard rubber ball and rebounded back the other way.

Norris thrust his pikestaff back in the direction he'd come from. It got stuck in something and he couldn't pull it out. There was a lot of whooping from somewhere behind me. Sally hadn't been able to do any homework for a week, and it sounded like she was making Mrs. Jones pay.

Then something barged into my right shoulder, knocking my trusty sword out of my hand. In a flash, I reached down for the dagger strapped to my ankle and lashed out at my assailant. After a few stabs at the air, the dagger buried itself in a large roll of skin.

Unfortunately, my hand followed it in.

With a huge effort and a big squelch, I managed to pull free. My arm felt wet. I looked at it, expecting it to be dripping with foul-smelling alien blood. It wasn't. It was worse than that. It was dripping with hot, salty, hamburger-smelling sweat. I doubled over, retching, and tried not to throw up all over the claymore, which had thankfully reappeared at my feet.

By now the smoke was starting to thin. I knew we only had a few seconds of cover left, so I swung the claymore back and forth wildly where I'd last seen the surprised face of Mr. Jones. There were some satisfying screams but still no blood as the sword just rebounded from one rubber ball-type thing to another.

Around me, I could now see Ms. Briars, Julie, and Sally swiping and stabbing at the aliens in the last wisps of the smoke. Norris joined us, having finally retrieved his pikestaff, and by the end, all five of us were in a perfect back-to-back circle of whirling steel. The bodies of our victims lay on the floor in front of us.

Sadly, as the smoke eventually cleared, we saw that none of them belonged to the right people.

Goran Sarta was crawling on his hands and knees trying to find the rest of his teeth. Peter Farrington and a bunch of other guys were clutching their stomachs and moaning. Sharon Stavely looked like she wasn't going to be able to play basketball for a while.

The rest had a variety of minor flesh wounds and were trying to fall back into their protective positions around Mr. and Mrs. Jones. It wasn't easy with the amount of sweat on the floor.

The Joneses didn't have a scratch on them.

"Bravo! Bravo! Encore! You know, I really didn't think the Drama Department could ever produce anything so entertaining. Oh, don't worry about them," Mr. Jones said, gesturing at his groaning bodyguards. "I have plenty more willing students. But I think I'd better have those now, don't you? Someone important might get hurt."

Suddenly Mr. Jones's head shrunk and his legs shriveled. The spare flesh shot into his arms, which tripled in length, and he snatched our weapons before we even had a chance to figure out what had happened.

It was like that cartoon, Mr. Tickle.

From your worst nightmares.

By the time he'd rearranged himself back to his normal hideous self, Mr. Jones's smile had vanished. Then he stretched his neck so that his triangular mouth was suddenly warm and wet next to my ear.

My ear wished it could move away as quickly.

"Do you know why I'm not going to eat you right now?" Mr. Jones whispered. He paused to let me answer. I didn't feel like it.

"Because I don't like you."

Mr. Jones's neck drew back in. He snapped his fingers and two of the bodyguards pushed in a cart loaded with cold and congealed hamburgers.

"If you don't feel like eating them now, don't worry," Mr. Jones said cheerfully. "I'm going to give you the chance to build up an appetite. You never know, I may even want to see you again when you're a little less skinny."

His mouth came over to my ear for one last pleasantry. "Let's see you write about this one, Jonny Jakes."

Then they left.

We heard them lock the door. Then we heard them board up the door. Then we heard them move lots of heavy things in front of the door.

Then all the lights went out.

You don't know what "pitch black" is until you've been locked in a drama studio and someone's turned off all the lights. We were all too shocked to speak at first.

Each one of us had just realized what complete and utter despair felt like.

It felt pretty horrible.

It wasn't long before the silence began to get to me. Every tiny sound was terrifying. I crouched down and started to run my hands over the floor around me. The more I felt nothing, the more I panicked. Finally, my hand met another hand. I heaved a giant sigh of relief.

Our two hands clung together. The other hand was smaller than mine, more delicate.

"Julie?" I whispered.

"No, it's Cynthia," Ms. Briars replied, patting my hand. "My, what warm hands you have."

For a minute, pitch black suddenly didn't seem so bad.

I'd just managed to pull my hand away when a blue light lit up Norris's face. He'd just remembered his cell phone in his pocket.

We were saved!

"No signal," Norris sighed.

We were doomed.

At least the phone gave us something to look at. Norris held it up and started to shine its light around the room. The shadows from the stage lights and the lighting bars were weird and seemed to move by themselves, but the walls and ceiling looked depressingly solid.

"I don't suppose there's another way out of here, is there?" Julie asked without conviction.

"I'm afraid not," Ms. Briars replied. "But I guess now is as good a time as any to clean out the props closet. Come on."

Ms. Briars crawled over to Norris, relieved him of his phone, and then made her way to the drama office. There were a few thumps and other looking-for-something type sounds. When she came out again, she was pushing a large box in front of her.

Most teachers have computers, textbooks, and unwashed coffee cups in their office. Ms. Briars has a secret stash of historical weapons and a big box of homemade scented candles.

It's a good thing Ms. Briars isn't like most teachers.

Before we lit anything, we found a black curtain and taped it around the edges of the door. Mr. Jones probably set guards outside and we didn't want them knowing we had light.

"What's this supposed to be?" Norris gasped as he lit the first one.

"Jasmine and tarragon," Ms. Briars informed us.

I'd never heard of jasmine and tarragon before, but as the smell invaded the room, I made a mental note never to set them on fire if I ever came across them again.

In the flickering light, we sorted the rest of the props into three piles: Useful, Possibly Useful, and Trash. There wasn't much to go in the Useful Pile. Mr. Jones had taken it all. There was a bow with no arrows, a catapult, and two really rusty swords.

Norris got excited when he found a set of machine guns in a box. Ms. Briars told him they were for some musical called *Bugsy Malone*. She said they were made from elastic bands and cardboard, and all they could fire was cream.

Norris was still really excited until he found out they weren't loaded.

We'd gotten halfway through the closet when we stopped for a break. Not only were the candles stinking up the place, they were hotter than I thought they'd be. I really needed a drink. Sally really needed something else.

That's when we remembered we didn't have a bathroom.

Then we started remembering all the other things we didn't have. Like food, electricity, or any hope at all.

And the rest of the day sort of went downhill from there.

Might be Tuesday

My pen's running out of ink. This will probably be the last thing I ever write.

I tried to sleep. I think some of the others tried too. But it's not easy when your bladder is bulging like a beach ball.

When sleeping didn't work, I tried to draw the glorious moment when me and Norris performed the Leap of the Double-Backed Tiger. It seemed like something that should be recorded for the ages.

But I'm not sure I captured Norris's good side.

Once you get used to the smell of the candles, another smell starts to creep into your nostrils: the smell of the hamburgers. They still smell absolutely disgusting — like a deep-fat fryer that hasn't been cleaned — but they also smell like food.

The moment I shut my eyes to try to sleep again, all I could see were hamburgers. Hamburgers piled high on a plate, hamburgers dancing with french fries, and hamburgers drinking ketchup. If my mouth wasn't so dry, I'd have been drooling.

This is depressing.

I'm going to stop now and concentrate on feeling sorry for myself.

I must have fallen asleep.

I woke up to the sound of the sky falling in. Or, as Julie put it, tons of fat kids all tromping around on the floor above us.

"What's going on?" Sally asked, clutching her aching stomach.

"Killer turnips!" Norris screamed as he woke up suddenly. His dreams must have been even weirder than mine.

Ms. Briars didn't say anything. I could just see her in the corner of the studio. She was sitting cross-legged, staring at nothing, and making a low humming noise. Either she was trying to meditate or the last remnants of her sanity were finally giving up on her.

"I'm desperate!" Sally moaned, reminding all of us about the no-bathroom situation.

"We've got to do something!" Julie whined, crossing her legs.

She was right, and just then I realized that maybe Mr. Hardy's assemblies hadn't been such a waste of time after all. If ever there was a time to "dig deep," "push the envelope," and "show some character," it was now. Someone needed to take charge. "Cometh the hour, cometh the man," had been another one of his favorite sayings. I didn't know what hour it was. I didn't even know what day it was, but I figured it was definitely time to cometh.

"Right. Norris, rip up the floor. If we're lucky, there might be some floorboards loose under the carpets; use a sword to lever them up if you have to. Sally, you check the walls. See if there are any gaps, weaknesses, anything! Julie, we're going through the rest of the props closet. We have to find something."

It's amazing what fear, panic, and really needing to pee can do. In two minutes, the studio was a wreck, and me and Julie had completely emptied the props closet. But there was nothing else to add to the Useful Pile.

We searched the office, too, but it was just four stupid walls with stupid old posters of stupid old plays.

One of them was for *Macbeth* so I ripped it off.

"What's that?" Julie asked.

"*Macbeth*!" I shrieked in fury, ripping the poster to pieces. "It won't leave me alone!"

"Not that. That!"

I looked up. Julie was pointing to where the poster used to be. There was a big square of wood where there should have been a brick wall.

I went and got a sword. Between us, me and Julie managed to get it under the edge of the wood and tear it loose.

Behind it was a big black hole.

I brought a candle over for a closer look. Julie called the others.

When I put the candle into the hole, the light flickered

on a stone wall in the back. There was nothing above but blackness. Looking down, I thought I could see the ground, but I couldn't be sure. To the right were two thick cords.

Sally and Norris came in. "You know what this is, don't you?" Sally beamed, looking over my shoulder.

We didn't.

"It's a dumbwaiter!" she explained.

That didn't help. She tried again.

"It's for lifting stuff up and down."

That was better.

Sally bets that before it became a drama studio, the room must have been some sort of food storeroom, so the dumbwaiter would have been used to transport food up to the kitchen.

She said dumbwaiters aren't called "dumb" as in stupid; they're called "dumb" as in silent.

This one wasn't.

As soon as Sally pulled on the cord, there was a horrible screeching, grating sound. Like someone playing a violin with a crowbar.

We froze and listened to the thuds on the floor above us. They seemed to be stomping around as normal, but we waited a few minutes until we spoke again, just in case.

"We'll have to wait until they're gone," Julie suggested.

"Or we could oil the bottom pulleys," Norris said, leaning over the edge of the hole. "I bet they're just down here. Do we have any oil?"

"Oh, sure," I replied. "Hang on while I just pull out the emergency oil can I keep in my pocket for exactly this type of scenario."

"I have a thing of chapstick," Julie said, giving me the evil eye. "It's not oil, but it's greasy. It might work. Can you reach the pulley?"

Norris strained himself to reach as far over the edge of the hole as he could. It wasn't a good move for someone with a full bladder.

"Not without leaving a puddle," he said, straightening back up and joining in with Julie on the evil eye. "If only there was someone we could dangle into the darkness head first, then we'd be all right."

No one appreciates my sense of humor.

Norris grabbed my legs as I walked my hands over the edge of the gap. He gradually lowered me down the dark shaft. My body shut out what little light there was, so I had to find the pulley by touch and then rub the chapstick all over it.

Once I'd been yanked back up, we gave the cord another try. Norris pulled slowly. The screeching had all but disappeared.

But as he pulled, we could hear another sound. A rumbling. I looked up and saw the top of the hole getting lower. In a few seconds, a box was descending from above, filling the space where the hole used to be.

"Now we just need a willing volunteer to test-drive it," Sally said cheerfully. She turned and looked at me. Norris and Julie joined in.

I wasn't allowed to take a candle with me because Julie thought it might set the waiter on fire. Sally agreed and added she was pretty sure that, in such a confined space, I'd soon be overcome by the fumes from the candle.

Norris didn't think it mattered whether I took a candle or not because the cord was so old that it was bound to snap before I got to the top, and I'd probably be dead from the fall anyway.

I gave Norris a gesture summing up how grateful I was for his concern.

If being locked in a drama studio without any light was scary, it was nothing compared to being pulled up in the dumbwaiter.

In seconds, my world was totally black and silent. The candlelight and the whispers of the others disappeared. It was horrible. My head told me I was going up, but my senses had nothing to prove it. I felt I was floating in a bottomless pit.

It was even more terrifying when I started to hear the creaking of the pulley at the top of the shaft. At any second, I expected to plummet to my doom. My stomach somersaulted in anticipation.

By the time the waiter stopped going up, I was curled into a ball of complete and utter terror.

I don't know how long I was like that. It might have been a few minutes. It might have been an hour. At last my survival instinct cut in. I had to stop myself panicking so I slapped myself.

Not easy in a confined space.

I told myself that if there was a way out of the shaft at the bottom, then there must be a way out at the top. I tapped the space in front of me. It was a wall. I started to panic again.

I forced myself to stop freaking out and assess the situation. I was too coiled up to be sure, but it seemed like there was light coming from somewhere. And if there was, that somewhere must be the way out. I tapped backward with my foot. Something wobbled and I let out a sigh of relief.

Another thing that involved a lot more effort than I expected.

Turning around was even harder and took me forever. But when I was done, I could see a tiny sliver of light at the bottom of whatever was in front of me.

It was the most wonderful thing I'd ever seen.

I put my fingers in the gap where the light was and lifted. Whatever I was holding started to roll up. I lifted it just enough to look underneath.

I was in the kitchen. There didn't seem to be anyone around, so I lifted the panel up a little farther.

It was night. I could see the blackness through the tops of the windows. The light was coming from the fire exit signs. It was a thin and watery light but enough to see by. I lifted the rolling panel higher so I could crawl out. It felt so good to be upright again. I gave the cord three tugs to let the others know they could come up.

It was freaky being in the kitchen. I'd sneaked around a lot of the school — it was part of the job — but I'd always been a little scared of the kitchen. Or, rather, I'd always been a little scared of the lunch ladies.

They didn't like one of my stories:

THE WOODFORD WORD

THE SLOPPY GLOP MUST STOP

In another attack on our taste buds, the school cafeteria has done it again. Following last week's rock-hard

My extreme close-up of congealed baked beans must have upset them. It upset everyone else. The whole school brought cold lunches for the next week.

The kitchen was full of stainless steel doors and shiny pans and sharp knives. The fire exit light was weak, but with all the reflective surfaces, it had a nasty habit of jumping out at you when you went around a corner. At the far end of the kitchen was a slightly open, large red door and through it I saw a slice of heaven.

A bathroom.

When I'd finished, I focused on my second priority: I needed food and something to drink, but before all that, I needed to find a new pen. After I did that, I filled a measuring cup with water from one of the sinks and gulped it down.

My stomach was so empty I heard the water hit the bottom.

I opened some cabinets to try and find some safe food. The first one was full of hamburger mix. So were the rest.

I was opening a fridge when a terrifying buzz zapped somewhere behind me. *FFZZZZAAACK!*

Instinctively I fell flat on my stomach and squashed my nose on the floor.

I lay there trying to figure out where the shot had come from. There had been no warning. The assassin was utterly silent. It was like being shot at by a shadow. I desperately wanted to sneeze, but I held it back, knowing that if I sneezed, I'd be doing it for the last time. My attacker didn't strike me as the sort of person to miss twice.

I strained every fiber of my being to hear a breath, a click, a footstep — anything to give me an idea of where they were lying in wait.

Instead, I heard a giggle.

I looked around and saw Julie's head popping up out of the dumbwaiter, laughing her head off at what I thought were my final moments.

That's girls for you.

"Hey," she whispered. "Over there." She pointed to the other side of the kitchen. I turned to look and saw a neon circle behind a wire grill. There was some writing next to it. It read: INSECTECUTOR.

I'd just been attacked by an electric fly zapper.

Once Norris and Sally were up, we continued our search for food. Nobody could get Ms. Briars to come up — she was still lost in her meditation. Norris found a can of baked beans that had fallen behind one of the stoves and hugged it tight. It was three years past its expiration date, but he was prepared to take the risk. Other than that, it was all burgers.

Julie couldn't understand it.

"Why are there so many of them? I mean, everyone's huge already and they can't eat everyone all at once, can they?"

The question hung in the air like a dirty pair of underwear. And, like a dirty pair of underwear, no one really wanted to think about it.

Norris summed up everyone's feelings. "Let's get out of here."

The main kitchen door was locked. Norris gave it a shove, but it wasn't going anywhere anytime soon. Julie tried the fire exit, but that didn't budge either. I could see that all the windows could open at the top, but they were padlocked shut.

Plan A wasn't looking good.

"We could always smash them," Norris suggested, pointing at the windows and picking up an extra large frying pan.

"Won't that make a lot of noise?" Sally said.

"So?"

"So are you sure we want to draw attention to ourselves?"

"Of course we want to draw attention to ourselves," I pointed out. "In fact, I think we could use some serious attention. I'm thinking police, firemen, the FBI, etc. And

I know just how to get it. You don't need to smash the windows, just one of these."

I jabbed my elbow into the glass of the nearest fire alarm and waited for the sweet sound that would mean help was on its way.

Nothing happened.

I looked at the glass to check that I'd broken it. Then I hit it again, just to make sure. There was a complete lack of ear-splitting noise.

Norris pointed out the reason. The cable that ran out of the fire alarm had been ripped out. I followed the trail of the ripped-out cable. It ended at a non-existent bell.

Just to add to the good news, Julie appeared out of Mrs. Trumpit's office with her telephone. Or what was left of it.

"And the computer's the same," she muttered.

"And my phone still can't get a signal," Norris said, checking his phone as it charged in one of the kitchen's sockets.

It looked like Mr. Jones was making sure he didn't get any unexpected visitors.

We went back to the windows and looked out gloomily. In the distance, there were lights on in the houses. Out there was electricity, TV, and food that wouldn't kill you. It was all too much. I picked up the nearest pot and hurled it at the window with a primal scream.

Then everyone else started screaming.

That was because the pot hit an invisible force field and disintegrated in midair.

"Code Red," screeched a piercing voice coming out of nowhere. Then it said it again and again and again.

"Time to go!" Julie commanded, heading for the dumbwaiter. "Ladies first, right, Sally?"

The girls started hauling themselves down as quickly as they could before Norris and I had a chance to argue. Norris called dibs on the next ride and pointed out that, being the biggest, he'd need the waiter to himself and I'd have to go last.

You find out who your friends are when it's Code Red.

I was taking some last-minute pictures of the fire bell for evidence when I heard footsteps outside. I rushed back over to the waiter, and as soon as Norris got out, I pulled like crazy to get the waiter back up in time.

A key started turning in the lock just as the dumbwaiter came up. Fortunately, the opening wasn't in direct view of the door, so I still had a few seconds. I was curling up on the shelf again just as the door opened.

With sweaty, shaky hands I tried to pull the panel door back down without making a sound. I still had four or five inches to go when a familiar voice bellowed, "Stop!"

So I did.

"Listen," Mr. Jones whispered. "I thought I heard something."

I realized then that he hadn't been talking to me. I had to close the last few inches before they got any closer. I tried to relax; one false squeak and we were all dead.

Inch by inch I slid the panel door down. When I couldn't see any more light, I stopped. But the danger hadn't passed. There was no way I could try to go back down with Mr. Jones still snooping around. The dumbwaiter still wasn't exactly quiet.

I waited and waited. I couldn't hear a thing, but with Mr. Jones sneaking around and the panel door shut, that was hardly surprising. A tiny draft came up from the bottom of the panel door.

I strained to hear the opening and closing of the kitchen door that would let me know I was on my own, but there wasn't a sound.

The tiny space was getting to me, and it was getting harder and harder to breathe. I put my face close to the gap and sucked in the thin trickle of cold air, but it wasn't enough and everything went black.

I woke up with a horrible sinking feeling in the pit of my stomach.

The dumbwaiter was going down.

Norris greeted me at the bottom. When I say "greeted me," I mean he screamed at me and thrust a sword in my face. His eyes were wild.

"Norris, it's me," I yelled, throwing my hands up to protect myself.

Norris brought a candle up to my face. I wished he hadn't. It smelled even worse than the other ones. When he was sure it was really me, his face relaxed a little and he lowered the sword. He was breathing unsteadily and looked completely exhausted.

He told me he thought I was dead.

I didn't quite know how to take it.

"Uh, well . . . apparently not," I tried, hoping I wasn't.

"When no one tugged on the cord, we thought you must be dead," he explained.

"Again, apparently not," I replied.

"We thought Mr. Jones would send someone down to trick us," Norris continued. "We thought he got you."

"Look, I get the idea, but I'm okay! I'm still alive." I breathed in and out exaggeratedly. "I just couldn't pull the cord because they'd have heard you pulling me down. I was waiting for them to go, but I think I fainted. Or maybe I fell asleep. How long was I up there?"

"No idea," Norris mumbled. "Phone went dead a while ago."

Painfully I uncurled myself and climbed out of the dumbwaiter. My legs were numb and it felt really weird to be upright. Norris helped me into the drama studio.

It was a grim scene.

Everyone was in their own little world of despair. Ms. Briars had given up meditating and, without her glasses on, looked twenty years older. Sally was sitting with her back to the hamburgers and drooling. Julie looked like she'd never slept in her whole life. They all smiled at me, but I could tell it took a huge effort.

I wondered again just how long I'd been asleep. How long had my companions been down here thinking I was dead and waiting for the final curtain?

Norris brought over an old metal helmet. It was upside down with a spike at the bottom. He put it in front of me and made a scooping motion with his hand. He was so tired he'd lost the power of speech. Job done, he headed for a quiet corner to collapse into.

There was something lurking at the bottom of the helmet; something that smelled funny and had a thick red crust on.

"Ms. Briars cooked the beans over the candle. We left you some," Julie explained. "Sorry."

When I tasted the beans I saw what she meant. These were not baked beans. These were baked beans with seriously weird stuff mixed in. My tongue struggled to make sense of it.

"Raspberry Essence and Chili Jam," Ms. Briars informed me as I gagged up the strange goop.

As disgusting as Ms. Briars had made them, the beans were still food and I forced some of them down.

"So, what's the plan?" I asked in between mouthfuls, trying to sound enthusiastic. "There is a plan, right?"

I looked around. Everyone else looked away.

"Oh. I see."

Even the baked beans couldn't hide the taste of defeat in the room. I tried to throw out some helpful suggestions, but none of them got beyond the "we could try . . ." stage before they found their own dark corner to collapse into.

All the party needed now was the Grim Reaper. Instead, Mr. Jones turned up.

As we heard the lockers being pulled away from the door, we half-heartedly forced ourselves to our feet and grabbed the remainder of Ms. Briars's weapons. If

Mr. Jones was going to kill us, he was going to have to fight us first. It wouldn't be much of a fight, but that wasn't the point.

It was almost worth seeing Mr. Jones again for the look on his face when he saw that we were neither fat nor dead. The same dark something I'd seen swimming at the back of his eyes during that assembly returned, and his chest started heaving.

His bodyguards kept close to him as he carefully inspected the hamburger pile. It was clear we hadn't touched it. He kicked the pile in frustration.

I couldn't take my eyes off his mouth. It was frothing with foul, acid-smelling spit. I hadn't seen Mr. Jones eat anything but candy and cookies since he'd arrived, but now it looked like he and his three tongues were finally

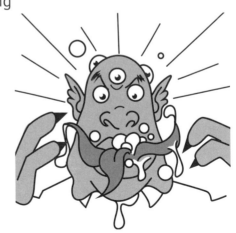

ready for dinner. I wondered what being licked to death would feel like.

It wasn't a smart thing to do.

With a deep breath, Mr. Jones recovered himself. He looked at how weak and exhausted we were. That seemed to cheer him up.

He waved his new bodyguards into action with a flick of his wrist.

"Have fun, children."

I charged at the nearest bodyguard, Kevin Hoyle, and swung a dull, rusty sword toward the rolls of fat where I thought his neck must be. Kevin Hoyle stepped aside and swung his fist to exactly where he thought my chin was.

The others didn't even have the energy to charge before they got smashed into a pulp.

As we lay groaning at his feet, Mr. Jones started to walk between us.

"A shame, really," he began. "I haven't had an adversary with quite so much . . . persistence for a long time. There was a troublemaker on Grar once who put up a bit of a fight, I remember. Of course, it made it all the more enjoyable when I crushed him."

On the word "crushed," Mr. Jones made sure that his middle foot landed on my outstretched hand. It stayed there as he carried on.

"But all good things must come to an end. That's one of your Earth sayings, isn't it? We don't have that on Huurl. It loses a little bit in translation, but our saying goes something like 'all powerful things will live for eternity by crushing the weak beneath them.' Not as punchy as some of your headlines, perhaps, but I think you'll agree it grabs your attention."

By carefully shifting the weight on his middle foot, Mr. Jones was breaking my fingers. One by one. I bit my tongue to stop myself from screaming.

"So, Jonny Jakes. We won't be seeing each other again. I shall miss our little chats, but I'll just have to console myself with visions of your imminent demise. I'm afraid you won't be able to make our celebratory banquet, but I assure you, your fellow classmates can't wait.

"And don't worry about all of your parents," he goaded, heading for the door. "They're particularly excited. They loved being in school today. They especially loved the food. Funny, they haven't mentioned any of you."

Mr. Jones was about to leave. I looked around, desperate for one last chance to hurt him. The bodyguards had found the Useful Pile and taken it. The only thing within my reach was the spiked helmet.

I hurled it with my good hand at Mr. Jones's grinning face. The helmet missed, but a tiny splatter of beans sprayed his cheek.

There was a pause as Mr. Jones's smallest and highest eye looked down and took in the tiny red stain.

He smiled and brushed the bean juice off.

Then he went crazy.

He started stomping up and down. His eyes watered and his cheeks puffed up. He was having some sort of allergic reaction.

He tried desperately to wipe the bean juice off his face and his fingers. Then his nose started to inflate. In seconds it looked like something that belonged on top of a steamship.

Then Mr. Jones sneezed.

A huge ball of yellow-green goo flew across the room and squelched against the wall on the far side of the drama studio. Mr. Jones screamed and held his head in agony. He wheeled on the spot like a demented demon.

So would you if you'd just sneezed some of your brains out.

Clutching his head, Mr. Jones staggered toward the door. I ran over and tried to scoop some more of the baked beans out of the helmet, but there was nothing left other than flaky crumbs that just stuck to my fingers.

As Mr. Jones left, he waved a hand at the various water pipes running along the bottom of the room.

"Rip them off," he commanded his bodyguards. "All of them!" he screamed.

Then he was gone.

The bodyguards didn't waste time in kicking the pipes to smithereens. I hadn't realized just how much water was running through the studio until it all started pouring out. It was a big room, but within seconds we were sloshing around in an inch of water. To make matters worse, we could hear a lot of noise in the hall.

A lot of blocking-the-door-so-everyone-in-the-studio-drowns kind of noise.

There was no time to talk about what we'd just seen. We headed right for the dumbwaiter and whatever waited above us.

Sally and Julie squashed in first again and were about to go up when Ms. Briars thought of something.

"Take these," she said, handing over some of the Tupperware containers me and Julie had cleared out of her office. Turmeric, Pineapple, and Paprika Paste; Cracked Black Pepper and Cinnamon Mix; and Nutmeg, Celery, and Garlic Surprise. "If there's any one up there, fire at will."

As soon as they went, Ms. Briars sploshed back for more highly flavored ammunition. I made sure my notebook stayed dry and tried not to think about the pain flooding up my arm.

When we got the three tugs on the cord, Norris let me go next. I wasn't going to be much good at pulling with only one working hand.

"It's all clear," Sally reassured me when I got up, then she went back to help yank on the cord.

It was nighttime in the kitchen again, and there was no sign of life.

Ms. Briars was last to come up. She was wet to the waist, but her top half was covered in dust. She had a large yellow box with her. The box had a big red cross and various warning stickers on it. Most of them said DANGER.

We waited for an explanation.

"I've been saving it for a special occasion," Ms. Briars said cheerfully.

When we'd all had a chance to use the bathroom and gulp down some water, we huddled down and whispered as quietly as we could.

"So what just happened down there?" Norris asked. It was a good question.

We established three key points:

1. Mr. Jones doesn't like Ms. Briars's cooking.

2. Our friends and family are all going to be eaten tomorrow.

3. Mr. Jones hasn't realized we can get into the kitchen.

"I got it!" said Sally, as if she'd just worked something out. "The hamburgers! He's more sensitive to things than we are."

"I hardly think trying to eat everybody qualifies as being sensitive," Ms. Briars argued.

"No. Not sensitive like that. Sensitive to strong flavors. That's why he's been feeding everyone those bland hamburgers. They make you fat, but maybe they tenderize you at the same time.

"He's sensitive to light, too," I said, thinking aloud. "Remember that time we first saw him?" Norris nodded. "He never goes outside without something protecting him from the sun."

"So we need to throw more food at him?" Norris summed up. "Especially If it's spicy, herby, and weird like Ms. Briars's stuff. No offense."

"None taken," Ms. Briars replied. "I suggest we spike the hamburger mix and work on ways of propelling it at Mr. and Mrs. Jones."

"What about the . . . that?" Julie pointed at Ms. Briars's big yellow box.

"All in good time," Ms. Briars purred as she gave it a stroke.

We split up. Ms. Briars and the girls started mixing extreme flavors into the hamburger mix. Norris and I started thinking about how to fire it.

The obvious thing was just to get a bunch of long-handled serving spoons and flick little balls of it. Norris wanted something a little more spectacular, though. I asked him what he was going to do with a bunch of cooking stuff and silverware. He said he wasn't quite sure yet, but he had a name already figured out: The Spatulator.

I left him to it and went to see if I could find any ice for my fingers.

I found a huge bag of frozen peas in the bottom of a freezer and wrapped it in a hand towel, then put it around my throbbing hand.

I explored some more. In the back of the kitchen, between the shelves of hand towels and tablecloths and a row of industrial-sized microwaves, there were tons of carts. They were parked in a long line and covered in crisp white cloths. They hadn't been there last time. I bet they were going to be used to get stuff to the banquet.

I'd found a way out of the kitchen.

One of the carts had a cake with WELCOME written on it in curly, frosting letters. I could smell rich, chocolaty fudge and hints of tart raspberry. The last thing I ate was so disgusting it made Mr. Jones's head explode and now, here I was, in front of a delicious cake that I knew I couldn't eat.

I did the only thing I could do.

I drooled.

"Over here," I whispered to the others as loudly as I dared. "Watch out for the puddle."

Everyone came to stare at the cake. It was enormous.

Ms. Briars was rubbing her hands in glee.

"What's up, Ms. Briars?" Norris asked.

She smiled. "I think I just found something special." Ms. Briars locked her fingers together and stretched them out in front of her like someone about to break open a safe. "Bring me my box."

As Norris and Ms. Briars worked on their weapons of mass destruction, the rest of us kept working on the hamburger mix.

There were three main jobs: Sally took the existing patties out of the fridge, put them into a mixing bowl, and added some of Ms. Briars's flavoring before forming them again, just slightly smaller. Julie was making ready-to-throw burger balls with the leftovers.

I supervised.

"Are you just going to stand there?" Julie asked as I wondered how everyone was going to like having their hamburgers spiked. I bet they were going to freak out.

"I have a bad hand."

"That still leaves your other hand. You could stir some of this into the sacks." She handed me a box of Rosemary and Fennel Fusion.

"It's serious. I'll never be able to clap my hands again."

"Not if you don't help out, you won't."

I took the hint and started pulling out three sacks of the dry hamburger mix from a cabinet. I poured Rosemary and Fennel Fusion into each sack and stirred it in with a long wooden spoon.

I'd gone through three more tubs of herbs when I got to the final cabinet in the row.

"Weird, this one's locked," I said, pointing it out to the others. "Which, come to think of it, is really weird, because it doesn't actually have a lock on it."

"It's glued shut," Norris said, looking closely. "I'll get a knife."

With a bit of persuasion, the glue around the cabinet door eventually gave up and Norris yanked it open.

Then the smell hit us.

It wasn't a bad smell — it was just powerful. Like someone had lifted the lid off a thousand spice bottles all at the same time.

We'd found where Mr. Jones had hidden all the flavor.

There were spices, there were purees, there were cartons. Mr. Jones wouldn't know what hit him.

It was a long night, but by the time we'd finished, we were armed to the teeth. Sally and Julie had spiked thousands of burgers and molded hundreds of burger balls packed with just about every flavor known to mankind. I'd made sure that any other fresh burgers made from the sacks of dry mix would be equally horrible. Norris had perfected The Spatulator and Ms. Briars had rigged up the cake so that one of the candles acted as a fuse for *The Big One.*

She explained that it was the ultimate in theatrical explosions and required a special license.

Norris asked if he could apply for one.

She also pointed out that, in addition to the force of the explosion, anyone near the cake when it went off would be hit with an extreme dose of curry powder.

When the first fingers of light showed in the sky outside, we cleaned up. We rearranged the carts so that five of them had space on their bottom shelves for us. Then we each took a pile of Julie and Sally's spicy burger balls, stuffed our pockets with anything else we might be able to throw, squeeze, or squirt at our enemy, and tried to make ourselves comfortable on the carts.

There's nothing left to do but hope we don't get discovered and try to get some sleep.

It didn't happen.

Half an hour later, the kitchen was throbbing with noise and activity. It seemed like the whole school was in there with us. When the burgers hit the frying pans, the smell was intense.

The carts shook all day long as fat footsteps pounded up and down. The carts vibrated so much we had to hug our weapons to our chests to stop them from jumping out onto the floor.

It would have been easier to sleep in a washing machine.

It was torture trying to stay hidden within the four white walls of the carts. My neck and shoulders felt like someone had tied knots in them. I must have tried hundreds of slightly different positions, but I couldn't get comfortable for even a second. I'd always thought having a limb fall asleep was kind of funny, but it's a pretty sick joke when it feels like your arm's going to fall off.

Even worse was not having the faintest idea what was going on. Although there were tons of people going in and out of the kitchen, not one of them said a word. There was just the thumping of feet, the clanging of pans, and the sizzling and spitting of frying burgers.

At some point during the day, I heard at least one cart being wheeled away. My whole body broke out into goose bumps thinking we were about to be discovered.

I tried to work on my Alien Survival Guide to take my mind off it all. It was good to finally have something to put in the "Weaknesses" section.

Alien Weaknesses:

 1. Sensitive to direct sunlight and any sort of criticism.

 2. Allergic to strong flavors and spicy food. Have been known to sneeze their own brains out.

However, by the time my cart finally started moving, I'd gone into some sort of trance. I was so tired and giddy I was starting to see things in the folds of the cloth. It had gotten to the stage where the little people had started talking to me.

If I had stayed in the kitchen any longer, I'd have started talking back.

The person pushing my cart was grunting with the effort. I just hoped they didn't start looking underneath to see why it was so heavy.

As the adrenaline kicked in, the fuzziness started to wear off. My hearing became hypersensitive. I strained for the sound of other carts. I could hear two sets of squeaking wheels super close to me and wondered who might be on them.

It wasn't hard figuring out when we'd gotten to the cafeteria. If the squelch of saliva hadn't given it away, then the gulp and swallow of hundreds of mouthfuls of half-chewed food cleared things up.

And still no one talked. Or if they did, they did it with their mouths so crammed full of hamburger that it was impossible to make out a word they were saying.

The tension became unbearable.

The plan was to wait until Mr. Jones had lit the candles on the cake. Once *The Big One* had done its worst, we'd burst out of our hiding places to finish off any parts of Mr. and Mrs. Jones that were left. After that, we'd have to see what kind of mood their minions were in.

It was a simple enough plan, but behind my cloth, I didn't have the faintest idea what was going on, and it was driving me crazy.

My ears started playing tricks on me. Every sound started to sound like Norris or Julie breaking cover or giving some sort of signal to attack. Then the voices started. One voice in my head told me to attack. Another voice told me to sit tight. A third voice asked me if I wanted cream with my coffee.

I told the little people they weren't helping.

I had to look.

My cart had been unloaded the minute it had arrived in the cafeteria and it hadn't moved since. I was sure everyone would be way too busy eating to notice me. All the same, I lifted the cloth up very carefully.

It was a relief to see a world beyond the tablecloth. Even if that world was full of people gorging themselves on hamburgers from Huurl. The cafeteria was lit by candles. They cast large, sinister shadows on the walls, but at least these ones didn't smell.

Every table was the same. In the center of each table was a rapidly disappearing mountain of burgers and around the edge were rapidly expanding mountains of kids and parents. Their manners had disappeared along with everything else, and everyone ate caveman style with greasy, greedy fingers.

I looked around for my parents. I couldn't see them anywhere. For a moment, I thought that somehow they had escaped. Then I realized I needed to be looking for much fatter versions of my parents. That's when I saw them. My stomach lurched.

They were as fat and vacant and doomed as everyone else. If anything, my dad was fatter.

At the front of the room was a podium and a table with a red and gold velvet tablecloth, presumably for the principal and his hideous wife, but there was no sign of them yet. In front of the table was one of the catering carts. I could tell by the cake-like shape beneath the cloth which one it was.

I pulled my head back under the cloth and waited.

I'd completely forgotten we'd spiked the hamburgers until I started hearing the screams.

Actually, "screams" doesn't really do the sound justice. It was more like something you'd hear if you tried to boil an elephant in a pressure cooker.

I had to take another look.

A cafeteria full of red-faced diners were clutching their stomachs and throats in pain. The spiked burgers had finally reawakened their taste buds, but their mangled brains were still telling them to eat. Their eyes were bulging out beyond their chubby cheeks.

No one was in any state to notice me, so I took the risk of looking out the other side of the cart. The scene was the same. I saw a twitch in the cloth of a cart across the room. I couldn't see who it was, but I knew what they were thinking.

Where were the Joneses?

The piles of hamburgers were growing smaller and
smaller. Some tables had eaten almost every single
one. The wailing and screeching had reached some sort
of peak and was beginning to fade into gentle moaning.

Everyone was enormous.

No one showed any signs of leaving their tables, but
if they had, I don't think they would have made it.
People were literally wedged fast in their chairs, their
enormous swollen stomachs heaving against the edges
of the tables.

Gradually a silence descended on the room. The
candlelight flickered, but it was about the only thing
that moved.

"Good evening, everyone."

Mr. Jones's mocking voice boomed suddenly out of
hidden speakers. If evil had a sound, that was it.

The hairs on the back of my neck stood up. The hairs on
the back of everything stood up.

"I trust you've all eaten well," Mr. Jones continued. I looked around and saw Mr. Jones standing at the podium at the front of the cafeteria. He smiled an ugly grin at his dinner.

"Thank you all for coming. Forgive me for not joining you for the first course, but I needed to build up my appetite for the main event. You see, this really is a special occasion. Not just for Woodford School, but for my family. You haven't met my family, have you?"

Mr. Jones was playing with his food.

"Well then, let's get acquainted. Ladies and gentlemen, boys and girls, please welcome my eldest son, Hoorraarg."

A smattering of feeble applause rippled across the room. I looked behind me and saw another complete copy of Mr. Jones take a place at one of the tables. The man on his right attempted to lift his head and smile a welcome, but it was a step too far and his cheek crashed back on the table.

Mr. Jones continued. "And how about a warm reception for my eldest daughter, Sherraall?"

One by one, each of Mr. Jones's seventy-three children appeared and occupied the spare seat that had been left at each of the seventy-three tables. The children all looked exactly the same. By the time the youngest daughter took her seat, no one was in any state to be doing any clapping. In fact, most of the room was asleep.

"Children, welcome. It's wonderful to see you." Mr. Jones's voice was now full of affection. "Your mother's right, we really should do this more often. You know what she says, 'a galaxy is full of stars, but nothing's home until it's ours.'"

The children chuckled politely. My blood ran cold.

"Now then, children, as usual your mother's been working on a version of a local delicacy to accompany your first meal here. I hardly need to remind you about the effort your mother puts into this kind of thing, so make sure you show your appreciation. My darling slotherings, we give you . . . cake!"

I remember clearly the chanting: "Cake! Cake! Cake!"

I remember clearly my horror as the Jones children pulled their vicious-looking silverware out of their chin sacks and started bashing it on the tables in unison.

And I remember clearly my whole body turning to ice when, just as Mrs. Jones joined her husband at the podium, I saw Julie's face peering out beneath the cloth of the cart with the cake on it.

After that, everything's kind of a blur.

Time stood still as Mr. Jones struck a match and brought it to the first candle on the cake. I could see

Ms. Briars's eager face poking out of the cart across the cafeteria from me. She couldn't see me and I could tell she hadn't spotted Julie. Julie couldn't see me either. She had no idea the cake had been moved to her cart.

As the candle flared, I forced myself back to life. I clattered out of the cart and started waving my hands and screaming like a crazy person. Seventy-three alien offspring wondered what kind of entertainment their parents had booked for the family reunion.

"Julie! Get out! The cake! It's right above you!"

Julie's face fell in horror and she tried desperately to get out of the cart, but her body seized up. She half stumbled, half fell out of the cart and tried to pull herself away with her arms.

She was about six feet away from the cake when it exploded.

I don't know why Ms. Briars thought she might need a special effect that could take out a small village, but *The Big One* lived up to its name.

It wasn't just the cake that exploded. Mrs. Jones, who had been standing right over it with a large knife, was blown apart and the whole hall was instantly coated in chocolate fudge, raspberry bits, and luminous alien guts. It brightened the place up.

In the smoke, where the cake and Mrs. Jones had once been, there was no sign of Mr. Jones or Julie. Unlike his wife, Mr. Jones had realized that something was wrong with the cart and had ducked down.

The blast woke everyone up. Whether it was because of the sheer force of the blast or the death of one of their torturers, I'm not sure, but the kids and parents looked different right away. Their eyes had lost that glazed-over look. They were staring at themselves and pinching the huge rolls of flab on their arms. You could see them wondering how it got there.

Mr. Jones's children were also staring and pinching themselves. But that was because their mom had just been vaporized.

Suddenly a hail of gray balls filled the hall. Norris had lifted the cloth off his cart and unleashed The

Spatulator. The spicy meatballs had the same effect on Mr. Jones's children as they had had on their dad. The room soon rang with the sound of painful alien sneezes.

Ms. Briars and Sally had also broken cover and were letting it rip with long-handled spoons.

I couldn't move. I just kept staring at the spot where I'd last seen Julie.

"Watch out!"

Norris's warning jerked me into what was left of the real world. I turned my head and saw a group of Joneses heading my way. They'd taken advantage of Norris reloading and had already cut off the route back to my cart.

"You're going to pay for what you did to our mother, Earthling!" the largest of them snarled. His arm shot toward my throat.

A clammy hand lifted me off the ground and squeezed. My brain screamed for oxygen. My arms flapped uselessly at the alien's thick purple hide. Jones Junior laughed. I couldn't tell if it was for dramatic effect or if I was tickling him.

I gave up struggling. A part of me knew this was always how it was going to end.

As my right arm fell limply back down, it brushed against my pocket.

My pocket full of tomato puree.

Looking back, it was probably a good thing that my brain was beginning to shut down. If it hadn't, it might have stopped me from squeezing the tube of puree with my broken hand. It hurt. It *really* hurt. But it didn't hurt me as much as a tube of tomato puree in the face hurt my attacker.

In a cafeteria full of screaming people, the scream was still loud enough for everyone to turn and look. Even if they did turn away again pretty quickly.

That's because brain juice was spraying their way.

Norris was soon laying waste to the alien mob once he'd reloaded The Spatulator, so I went back to looking for Julie.

The smoke around the stage was finally clearing.

I could make out the cart that the cake had stood on. It was scorched but still standing. There was also a huge hole in the ceiling. The force of the explosion must have mainly gone upward.

There was a chance Julie had made it.

I called her name again and again. Eventually I got a reply.

"Hggggffffuuummmpph."

I moved toward the sound of her muffled voice.

"Julie, I'm here. Are you okay?" I asked.

Julie didn't reply. I realized why when I saw Mr. Jones emerging from the shadow of a darkened corner. It's hard to reply when your face is stuck under the leathery arm of an alien scumbag.

Mr. Jones looked different.

He had a chair leg through his knee.

We stared at each other, each of us weighing our next move. I had a deadly meatball in my hand. He had Julie.

"Persistent enough for you?" I asked.

"Don't think I won't," Mr. Jones replied, opening his mouth and pushing Julie toward it. "She may be tough and tasteless, but I'll do it. Put the meatball down and you might just get your girlfriend back."

"Put her down and I might just let you walk away," I replied.

I was trying to be cool, but it wasn't very convincing. I was shaking all over.

He'd just called Julie my girlfriend.

Julie caught my eye. I tried to make a gesture that showed her that all this talk about girlfriends had nothing to do with me. She made a gesture that showed me that she had a tube of garlic paste in her pocket and I needed to keep Mr. Jones talking.

"So . . . um . . . ," I tried.

But Mr. Jones wasn't in the mood for small talk. Ms. Briars, Sally, and Norris were obliterating the remainder of his children, and he was in the mood for revenge.

"Put down the meatball or I'll eat her. You have to the count of three. One, two . . ."

My brain froze. My mouth flapped uselessly up and down. Now that someone's life depended on it, I couldn't think of a thing to say.

So I started singing.

Mr. Jones stopped counting. In fact, after a few seconds, the whole room stopped what they were doing.

It was that bad.

I don't know why, but the first song that had come into my head was "Twinkle Twinkle Little Star." It was so, pathetic Mr. Jones couldn't resist flinging his head back for a final, victorious laugh.

It was a bad move.

In one swift move, Julie grabbed the tube of garlic paste, twisted off the cap, and sprayed it right into Mr. Jones's gaping jaws.

I stopped singing and there was silence as all eyes turned to Mr. Jones.

For a second or two, nothing happened. Then it didn't happen for another couple of seconds. Mr. Jones swallowed with a bemused look on his face. To everyone's surprise, it looked like the danger had passed.

Then Mr. Jones blew up.

I felt truly sorry for the janitors.

I rushed over to where Julie lay in a crumpled heap.

She was covered in a thick, sticky coating of foul-smelling gunk. I pulled her to her feet and asked her if she was okay. She said that apart from needing to spend all of next year in a bath, she was fine.

Among the gunk and the smoke and the smell of a thousand spice racks, I saw Norris, Sally, and Ms. Briars coming over to join us. The last of the Jones children had been taken care of, courtesy of a well-aimed pot of garam masala.

We looked at each other. We looked at the scene of devastation around us.

Then we headed for the exit.

I stopped at the pay phone by the main office and dialed nine-one-one.

The operator wanted to know which emergency service I required. I didn't know where to start.

"Just send them all down to Woodford School," I said.

"But I need you to tell me the nature of the incident," the operator complained.

"Trust me. You wouldn't believe me if I did."

"At least tell me your name, please."

"I don't think so. I've done way too much of that recently."

"But sir . . . ," the operator started whining.

"Listen, just get everyone here now! I have a deadline to meet, and this time I'm not going to miss it. If you really want to find out what happened, you'll have to do the same thing as everyone else tomorrow morning."

"What's that, sir?"

"Get a paper."

WORLD EXCLUSIVE

SPICE KNOWING YOU

Last night the world said goodbye to some unwanted
visitors in the biggest food fight ever recorded

EXCLUSIVE INTERVIEW

NAME:
Malcolm Judge

PROFESSION:
Author and teacher

BIO:
Malcolm Judge is a drama teacher in Cumbria, England.
He enjoys cycling, skiing, and making stuff up. He invented
Jonny Jakes so he could be rude and get away with it.

Describe your book in one sentence.
Jonny Jakes offends pretty much everyone, but on the
plus side, he does save the world from an evil alien.

Would you have joined Jonny's resistance group or would you not have been able to resist the candy . . . ?
I'm not good at saying no to sweets.

Do you think any of your teachers were secretly aliens?
No. Aliens would have had better clothes.

What was your favorite book as a kid?
The Hobbit by J.R.R. Tolkien. I've always loved adventure stories and the success of the underdog. As a young adult, my favorite book was *Catch-22* by Joseph Heller. It was mad, bad, and I couldn't put it down.

What is your favorite book now?
The Adventures of Huckleberry Finn by Mark Twain. I just loved the incredible voice of Huck and the whole romance of the epic raft journey.

How did you start writing?
I always loved writing at school. My school did a mini-newspaper that went in the local newspaper. It was called *The Willowbank Warbler* and I did some sports reports. My first taste of success was getting picked for the final fifteen of a national writing competition.

What's your typical writing day?
I usually write twice a week for two to three hours
each time.

What inspired you to write your book?
Jonny Jakes began life as a space pirate! I think the idea
was simply to put two things together that I knew my sons
would find interesting and see what happened.

What other jobs have you done?
Quite a few! Waiter, tree surgeon, and care worker to name
three. I am currently a teacher, but when I grow up I want
to be an international film star.

**What do you hope readers will think when they read
your book?**
I hope they laugh — a lot — but I also hope it will inspire
the rebel in them and get them thinking about how to
make a difference in their own world.

Is there anyone you would like to thank?
Penny West, my editor. This would not have happened
without her.

EXCLUSIVE INTERVIEW

NAME:

Alan Brown

PROFESSION:

Illustrator

BIO:

Alan Brown's love of comic art, cartoons, and drawing has driven him to follow his dreams of becoming an artist.

His career as a freelance artist and designer has allowed him to work on a wide range of projects, from magazine illustration and game design to children's books. He's had the good fortune to work on comics such as *Ben 10* and *Bravest Warriors.*

Alan lives in Newcastle, England, with his wife, sons, and dog.

Who's your favorite character to draw?
Without a doubt, Mr. Jones.

Who's your favorite character overall?
Jonny — nothing stops him from getting to the truth.

Would you have joined Jonny's resistance group or would you not have been able to resist the candy . . . ?
I'm not a great fan of sweets, so I could have resisted. If they were alien pork pies, that would be a different story.

Do you think any of your teachers were secretly aliens?
Some of my teachers were almost certainly aliens, but others were so much worse than that.

What was your favorite book as a child?
My favorite books were *The Twits* by Roald Dahl and a huge book on English folklore and myths my parents had. That's still my favorite book — it's really interesting to see where our traditions and beliefs come from.

How did you start illustrating?
I first got into illustration through doing storyboards for an ad agency. After many years working in graphic design, I've finally come back to my love of drawing. I've enjoyed

working on a great many jobs over the past few years, but the highlights are definitely drawing the *Ben 10 Omniverse* comics and, of course, working on *Jonny Jakes*.

Do you sketch by hand or digitally?
It all depends on deadlines. If it's a tight timescale, I work completely digital. But if I have the time, I prefer to draw traditionally, then work up the sketch digitally to create the final piece.

If you weren't an illustrator, what would you be and why?
Other than working as an illustrator, I've been a graphic designer and tattoo artist. But as a child I always wanted to be one of the guys who works in the lab for James Bond, making rocket pens and invisible shoes.

What's your typical working day?
I usually get up at 4:30 a.m., grab a coffee, and start work. At 6:30 a.m., I walk the dog and make breakfast, then generally go back to work at 9 a.m. and work through until about 6 or 7 p.m. Long days, but I get paid to draw aliens . . . can't complain!

THE WOODFORD WORD

WORLD EXCLUSIVE!
NEW PRINCIPAL IS AN ALIEN!

Meet Jonny Jakes, undercover reporter for banned school
newspaper *The Woodford Word*.

**Nothing will stop his pursuit of the
truth. Not teachers. Not parents.
Not even detention.**

When a new principal arrives halfway
through the semester, Jonny smells a
rat. Teachers handing out candy?
All-you-can-eat hamburgers?

He's determined to get to the
bottom of it, because Jonny Jakes
investig...   ...ts his

*definitely
<u>NOT</u> human*

*Mom's cooking
or alien drool?*

$8.95 US • $9.95 CAN

ISBN 978-1-4965-2680-9

50895

9 781496 526809

DBE991501

capstone
www.mycapstone.com